# *Saving Grace*

## (Book II in the Moon Island Series)

# Jennifer Fulton

*Yellow Rose Books*

Nederland, Texas

ISBN 1-932300-26-0
Second Edition

First Printing 2004

9 8 7 6 5 4 3 2 1

Cover design by Donna Pawlowski

Published by:

Yellow Rose Books
PMB 210, 8691 9th Avenue
Port Arthur, Texas 77642-8025

Find us on the World Wide Web at
http://www.regalcrest.biz

Printed in the United States of America

Acknowledgments:

My long suffering family knows how much I depend on their support. I am also indebted to Katherine V. Forrest and Christine Cassidy for their mentoring and editorial guidance as I worked on the first edition of this novel. More recently, I thank Lori L. Lake for her affable editing support on this second edition.

To Greenpeace and the countless environmental activists in New Zealand, Australia and the Pacific for their courage and persistence. The pristine world in which I grew up remains a paradise because ordinary people stood up against powerful interests.

# MOON ISLAND

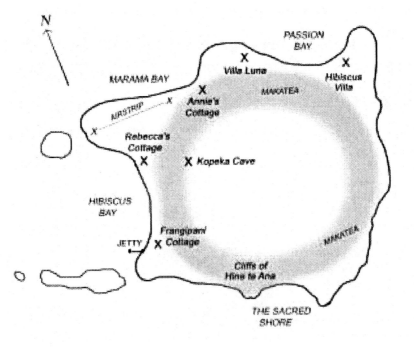

# Chapter
# One

IT WAS A typical Sydney summer's day. Beneath a tyrannous sun, the harbor milled with pleasure craft bearing such clichéd names as Pussy Galore or Freudian Slip. Their decks were plastered with basking socialites and hunky dark-haired waiters, and, trailing raucously in their wakes, gulls squabbled over the occasional jettisoned olive or stunned fish.

The Sydney Opera House, Holy Grail of countless camera-happy tourists, loomed against a postcard sky. On the Manly Ferry, locals yawned over cans of Foster's, and a whimsical breeze toyed with the long, soft hair of a brace of truant schoolgirls.

Rearranging her own blond ponytail, Dawn Beaumont glumly surveyed the scene. "I'm bored," she declared.

"Is that all?" Her cousin, Trish, studied her with a hint of exasperation.

"Isn't it enough?"

Trish heaved a sigh and dug around in her handbag, producing a handful of tissues.

Dawn pushed them away. "Oh, what do you care! It's not your life." Tears slithered beneath her sunglasses.

"Don't be silly. Of course I care." Trish placed the tissues in Dawn's hand, pausing as her cousin mopped her face. "I know it's frustrating, but injuries like yours don't heal overnight."

"Frustrating! That's the understatement of the year. It's driving me 'round the bend living at home. Mom keeps on stuffing me full of pasta, and Dad won't shut up about me swimming in a goddamned disabled team. And there's all the trophies." Dawn blew her nose fiercely. "They won't put them away. I've asked."

"Give them time, Dawn. They need to come to terms with everything too."

"You make it sound like I'm dead. I bloody deserve to be." Dawn gazed at the water churning over the ferry's bow. Ordinarily she loved the trip across the harbor, the air so clean and salty, the hum of the city drifting discordantly across the water. But these days nothing gave her pleasure. Her life was ruined.

"Dawn." Trish's voice held a hint of rebuke. "We've already had this conversation. It's been six months since the accident." She glanced at Dawn's legs and looked quickly away. "You've got to stop blaming yourself."

"It *was* my fault."

"We all make mistakes. I think you've paid for yours."

"Well, some people wouldn't agree!" Since the accident she'd heard it a million times. *You were so lucky. It was a miracle.* And somewhere, lurking behind the forced brightness, that unspeakable question: *How come you survived and Lynda was killed?* By rights it should have been the other way around. Lynda was younger, an even better medal prospect for the Olympic squad. And she was sweet, gentle, and kind—everything Dawn wasn't.

Tears plopped off Dawn's chin onto her hands. "They all think it should have been me. They—"

"Now hold on," Trish protested. "That's simply not true and you know it! Everyone wants you back on your feet." She broke off, clearly pained by her own insensitive choice of words.

"Well, don't hold your breath!" Dawn kicked the walking stick propped beside her. "Just look at me, leaning on this bloody thing like a granny. I'll never swim again." She choked back a sob. Trish must be sick of the sound of her by now. All she ever seemed to do these days was cry.

But Trish took her hand. "You need some time out, away from all of this. From your parents and the reporters and everything. You need to get away from Sydney, go someplace where you can think. Take my word for it," she insisted as Dawn began a protest. "A change is as good as a rest. Besides, it's time you started planning your future.

"I don't have a future. My life is over."

"Nonsense!" Trish gently shook Dawn's shoulders. "You're only twenty-two. Of course you have a future. You won't be swimming in the Olympics, but neither will most of the population, and I think we'll survive."

"You don't understand," Dawn said sullenly.

Trish ignored her. "It's decided then. I'm going to book a holiday for you, a long way from here. I know the perfect destination."

"No. Absolutely not." Dawn had a bad feeling that she knew

just the place her cousin had in mind.

Somehow over the years, she had fallen into the habit of doing exactly what Trish wanted. In many ways Trish substituted as the big sister Dawn had never had. Almost ten years older, she had been a fixture in the Beaumont household, babysitting Dawn throughout her childhood and spending vacations with the family. No matter what Dawn did, Trish was always on her side, encouraging her to do better, protecting her when she needed it.

Already she was acting as if Dawn had agreed to everything. "You're going to love it," she promised.

"Trish, I said no." It might have been easier to sound resolute if the idea of getting out of Sydney weren't so appealing.

"But you meant yes." Trish was already consulting her Palm Pilot, no doubt finding her travel agent's number. "Darling, it's written all over your sad little face. Why fight it?"

"I suppose you're talking about that rotten island."

Trish was wreathed in smiles. "Well, you had such a ball last time with the hurricane and everything..."

GRACE RAMSAY OPENED her eyes and lay frozen between the sheets, a shrill sound rising from her throat. What should have been a scream was just a sigh, escaping from her lips like gas from a soda bottle. With a concentrated effort, she moved first her hands, then her feet. Then she waited. For what, she was uncertain.

*The Dream.* With shaking fingers, she touched her face. Her skin was clammy. She examined her hands, unsure what she expected to see. In the wan first light, they were pale and unsullied. They dropped to her chest and nestled there.

Grace stared around the hotel room. Bland, uncluttered walls stared back. A full-length mirror gaped on the opposite wall. Abandoning her bed, she drifted toward the tall copper-haired woman reflected there. Dark, shadowed eyes met hers, the pupils huge. For a moment, something flickered in them, the shock of some horror freshly witnessed. Grace gazed intently, willing memory to surface, but there was only that familiar blankness, a sense of groping in the dark for a phantom. She turned away, gathered up some clothes, and retreated to the impersonal solitude of her bathroom.

A FEW HOURS later, she was in the downstairs bar knocking back Margaritas and listening absently as the band mutilated a Springsteen song. She detested drinking alone in hotels, evading the calculating eyes of men on the prowl. Worse still, she hated competing with them for women to chat up. Layovers were the pits. If only she had been able to change planes and fly out of L.A. yesterday. But Robert B. Hausmann himself had insisted on seeing her before she left for the Cook Islands.

Drumming her fingers, she drained her glass and signaled for another drink. It was not like the CEO of Argus Chemco to be late. She wondered how far her boss had got with the Moon Island deal. The owners hadn't shown much interest when they were initially approached. But in Grace's experience, there was more than one way to persuade people that signing on the dotted line was a smart move. Hausmann played to win. He had not built a billion dollar global dumping operation by being a wuss.

It wasn't easy to find an optimum location for toxic waste disposal these days. Although the U.S. had stymied the passage of rigorous global restrictions at the Basel Convention in 1989, and despite the most ineffectual international policing, third world countries were getting increasingly tetchy about foreign shipments. Of course, thanks to bribery, corruption, and the hefty financial incentives Argus could offer co-operative governments, they could always fall back on the usual suspects—China, India, Pakistan, Brazil. But it wasn't that simple. For a company taking a long term view, there were all kinds of factors to consider—proximity to habitation, strategic and/or political importance, labor costs, media scrutiny, enforceability of any local environmental protection laws.

It was one thing for a host government to ignore the human rights of its citizens, quite another for a company like Argus to find its operations attracting the kind of negative publicity that had closed down the Colbert brothers in the 1980s. The Colbert's problem was greed and short-term thinking, Robert Hausmann was fond of saying. If you're going to ship millions of tons of phosphate, asbestos, uranium, DDT and PCBs all over the planet, you need to pay attention to the letter of the law.

God knows, there were enough loopholes to ensure toxic waste could easily be exported out of the U.S. The federal government, a big customer, had seen to that. No one needed to use phony labels or convoluted falsifications of shipping records. And it was just plain common sense not to get sloppy at the other end. Who needed an international incident like Nigeria?

Thanks to a bunch of leaking barrels that had originated in Italy, the Nigerian president had not only ordered the Italian government to take back the waste, but he also instituted the death penalty for waste traders. Until that fiasco, Africa had been an ideal dumping resource. Now, the place was barely viable. Argus avoided it like the plague. There were more dependable regions—the South Pacific, for one.

A remote, privately owned island was a waste dumper's dream come true—no inhabitants, no road access, no nosy reporters, no avaricious local bureaucrats needing constant payoffs to shut up about birth deformities. Hausmann had been hunting for the right site in the region for more than a year, and he had hit the jackpot with Moon Island.

Idly, Grace stirred her drink. The dumping contract could be worth hundreds of millions to the Cook Islands, and it sounded like their Premier was hot for the Argus proposal. Who could blame the guy—responsible for some flimsy banana republic economy totally dependent on foreign currency earnings. The only obstacle would be the island's owners. But everyone had their price, and Argus was willing to pay serious money for the right deal.

"Dr. Ramsay?"

Grace tensed as someone spoke her name. A woman with a briefcase stood opposite her. Somewhere in her thirties, black wavy hair to her shoulders, she had smooth olive skin and a body to die for.

With an appreciative smile, Grace said, "You're speaking to her, and it's Grace, by the way."

The delicious stranger shook her hand briefly. "I'm Camille Marquez, Robert Hausmann's assistant. Mr. Hausmann sends his apologies. He was called back East."

"Delighted to meet you." Grace wondered what had happened to Hilda Gruber, Hausmann's usual defender. Indicating a chair, she offered, "Can I get you a drink?"

"Martini, thanks." Camille's skirt tightened across her thighs when she sat. She had great legs and crossed them like she knew it, feet slightly to one side to set off her perfectly toned calves.

When Grace returned from the bar, Camille delved into her briefcase, extracting an envelope and handing it over. "The latest briefing papers for the Moon Island project."

Grace tore open the envelope and scanned the contents. The purchase of Moon Island seemed likely, but negotiations were, of course, sensitive at this stage. Grace's assessment of the island was to be carried out with the utmost discretion. She was to confirm as soon as possible the suitability of the site and the likely scope and time frame of the necessary site preparation. Hausmann was presently in negotiations with an important new Japanese client. The sooner he could offer a firm commencement date for dumping activities, the better.

"When is Mr. Hausmann leaving for Rarotonga?" Grace inquired.

Camille consulted her Filofax. "He has a meeting arranged with the owner of Moon Island in four days."

That would give her a chance to make a quick preliminary evaluation of the site. "Tell him I should be able to indicate viability by then," Grace said. "It won't be a definitive report, of course."

"I'll let him know." Camille was busily penning. "Mr. Hausmann will also be interested in any insights you might offer on the owners."

"I'll do my best. This Ms. Worth—do you have her first name?"

"Annabel."

Grace paused. "Funny, I knew an Annabel Worth years ago. Not the same person, I'm sure." The Annabel Worth she recalled would not be caught dead more than five miles from the nearest Neiman Marcus, let alone operating some ideologically right-on retreat for women only. She almost laughed at the idea.

The enchanting Camille closed her memo pad and uncrossed her elegant legs. "I'm here until tomorrow, Dr. Ramsay. Please let me know if I can be of any further assistance." The invitation in her tone was unmistakable.

A bisexual on the prowl. Grace smiled languidly. She could do worse. "Er... do you have plans for this evening?" she asked.

# Chapter
# Two

"WELL, HERE WE are." Trish humped Dawn's bags onto the check-in scales. "You okay?"

"Of course I am," Dawn said peevishly. She wished people would quit asking her that. They only did it out of guilt because they were relieved she was the cripple and not them.

Scanning the faces around her, she caught strangers looking hastily away. When you were young and limped along with a walking stick it changed everything. People either stared or pretended you weren't there. You couldn't go to a bloody barbecue without some fool wanting to put a blanket on you. In summer, for God's sake.

Even now, Trish was interrogating the ticketing clerk. Where would she be sitting in relation to the bathroom? No she couldn't stagger all that way up and down the aisles. What if it was a bumpy flight? Dawn prodded her and said it didn't matter, but Trish shoved a boarding pass into her hand with the pointed comment that the disabled are people, too.

"Maybe I shouldn't go," Dawn said miserably as they waited for her boarding call.

Trish laughed. "I see you're determined to have a lousy time."

"I am not!"

"Then cheer up, angel. And don't worry about your parents. I'll handle them."

Dawn cringed. Her parents had no idea about this expedition. They thought she was going away for a weekend yoga retreat in the Blue Mountains. As if! Dawn could hardly bear to contemplate their reactions when they found out what she was really up to. Since the accident, it was all they could do to let her use the bathroom by herself. They would have a cow over foreign travel.

Trish patted her hand. "If it makes you feel any better, at least they won't be able to contact you out there."

Dawn's jaw dropped a notch. She had forgotten how primitive Moon Island was. "You mean they still haven't got proper phones?"

"Just those crank-handle party lines," Trish said cheerfully. "Great, isn't it? Peace and quiet guaranteed."

The prospect was not exactly balm to her troubled spirits, Dawn reflected nine hours later as she hovered outside what passed for Rarotonga International Airport. She was hot and tired, and an announcement had just come over the pager that the Moon Island connection was running late. Typical!

Dawn slouched grumpily against her luggage. It was probably the same wreck of a plane as last time, too. Perhaps it had crashed en route. Ineffectually licking her dry lips, she dragged her sun hat lower. She was a fool to have come back here. She should never have allowed Trish to talk her into it. After the last time you'd think she might have learned her lesson. What a disaster that was. Normally, she would never have holidayed in a place like the Cook Islands. Her idea of a perfect destination was Queensland, where everyone ignored the beach and swam in hotel pools so they didn't get sand in their pants.

But back then, Trish had already booked and paid for the vacation to Moon Island. She'd had to cancel at the last minute when she landed some big photography contract at Ayres Rock and had offered Dawn her tickets. It had sounded great—a tropical island, luxury villas, golden beaches. The sneaky bitch hadn't said anything about the place being run by weirdos who only let women stay there.

It had been two weeks of relentless boredom. No phones, no electricity, no night life, and no men. To top it all off, a hurricane had hit the island and everyone was forced to spend two terrifying nights in the next best thing to the Batcave with some smartass Kiwi playing the Girl Wonder.

Cody Stanton. The mere thought of her made something crawl in the pit of Dawn's stomach. She could still picture that wretched woman loping along the jungle paths with that own-the-world walk. Who did she think she was, anyway?

Unzipping her cabin bag, Dawn rummaged crossly for her painkillers. Her legs ached from the flight. Pain was to be expected, the surgeon had said when he removed the plates and screws. An unstable comminuted fracture of the tibia and fibula, compound femoral fractures that had shattered both legs. She was lucky she could walk at all.

Dawn steered her mind in another direction. She didn't want to think about her ugly, useless legs. She just wanted to get to her destination and lie down. Where the hell were these people anyway? Didn't they want visitors? Fuming, she paid a kid two bucks to mind her luggage and hobbled indoors to buy herself a can of Coke. She snapped the tab viciously, dropped a couple of painkillers and guzzled the contents.

The boy and her bags were still there when she returned, and for a moment Dawn was almost sorry. If they had vanished, she would have had the perfect excuse to return home. But no. God wasn't doing Dawn Beaumont any favors this week. Sinking onto the nearest bench, she extended her legs, gently massaging her thighs and waiting for the pain to subside.

To her frustration, Cody Stanton's face hovered persistently in the foreground of her mind, dragging Dawn back in time to that final day on Moon Island three years before. After the hurricane, a group of guests had been at Villa Luna, the main house, waiting to be rescued by the cargo boat. Dawn had gone for a walk on Passion Bay, only to find Cody there with Annabel Worth, the woman who owned the island. They were in each other's arms, kissing exactly like lovers.

Dawn had taken one long mortified look and fled. Cody Stanton was a lesbian, she'd realized stupidly. For some reason the knowledge still made her knot up inside.

"Dawn?" A voice made her jump guiltily. "Is that you?"

A pair of long, neatly muscled legs stood before her. Dawn followed them up past slim hips and an ancient Levi's shirt, to a wide mouth and a pair of candid gray eyes. Cody hadn't changed a bit. "Of course it's me," she snapped. "I've been dying out here wondering when you'd bother to turn up."

Cody grinned, no sign of remorse. "Hey, it's great to see you, too. Must say, you're the last person we expected back here for a return visit. Are these all yours?" She nudged Dawn's luggage with her toe.

Jerking a brief nod, Dawn snatched up her stick and wobbled to her feet. Chin jutting, she dared Cody to make something of her condition.

But the taller woman tossed the luggage onto a cart as if eighty pounds weighed nothing, and strolled off across the heat softened tarmac. "Follow me," she called over her shoulder. "It's not far."

*What a bitch!* She might have had the decency to shorten her stride or check if her guest was okay. But no, she barely seemed to have noticed Dawn's predicament. Glaring after her, Dawn muttered a series of profanities beneath her breath, words her parents thought she didn't even know. It felt good. She was sick of censoring everything she said just so they could congratulate themselves on having brought their daughter up right.

By the time they reached the small, tatty-looking silver

plane Dawn remembered from her last visit, she was puffing with exertion and resentment. Firing a suspicious glance toward the hangar, she demanded, "Where's your pilot?" Surely they weren't going to roast out here for the next few hours waiting for some patch-up job. She remembered those running repairs all too well.

"Bevan's on holiday," Cody replied blandly. "Annabel's flying the shuttle."

"Terrific," Dawn sniffed, watching Cody stow the bags. *Amateurs.*

Finishing her task, Cody waved to someone. Turning automatically, Dawn faced a stunning platinum blond who looked as if she'd just walked off the pages of Vogue. Annabel Worth, the owner of Moon Island, the woman Cody lived with and kissed on the mouth like it didn't matter that anyone could see them.

"Dawn." Annabel removed her sunglasses and smiled warmly. "I'm so glad you've come back."

Mumbling a hello, Dawn tried not to be startled by Annabel's porcelain skin and her strange, pinky-lavender eyes. You got used to it when you saw her every day, but it was a bit of a shock after all this time.

"Let's get out of this heat." Annabel tossed her sun hat into the rickety plane, and pulled a decrepit leather flying jacket over her linen shirt. Helping Dawn aboard, she commented—as if Dawn were interested, "The Dominie's going like a rocket. We bought a Rapide for spare parts last year and Bevan's in England now, shopping for a couple of new motors for us."

Dawn shuddered. "I don't know why you don't just buy a whole new plane, instead of trying to keep this old wreck in the air."

Waiting for her to get seated, Cody looked like she was about to lose her temper. Annabel was obviously soppy over the stupid plane and maybe they couldn't afford a better one. Dawn hadn't meant to be tactless, but she was fed up. Besides, it was ridiculous to run a resort and not have a nice modern plane to transport your guests. She wriggled in her hard little seat, a stabbing queasiness rolling through her gut. The painkillers. She'd taken them on an empty stomach. The warm Coke probably hadn't helped either.

Annabel started the plane and Dawn stuck her fingers in her ears, wishing she could block out the desperate whine of the engines, the foul petrol fumes and the jarring vibration. It would also be nice if Cody Stanton wasn't sitting so close she was virtually in Dawn's lap. Twisting to see if there was an empty seat behind her, Dawn groaned. There were four, but each was jammed with supplies.

The plane lurched. Bracing herself, she closed her eyes. If they were going to end up in the drink, she didn't want to watch. Several teeth-rattling minutes later, one of her hands was pulled away from her ear and Cody's voice said, "It's safe to look now."

Dawn could not conceal a slight start at the contact. Bestowing a dirty look on the dark-haired New Zealander, she made a point of gazing out her window. They were airborne and the propeller noise had tapered off to a bearable thrum. She couldn't help but marvel at the blue infinity below. But for the hint of whitecaps, the ocean seemed inseparable from the sky. There was no sign of land on the vast, curved horizon. The sun sat high above, gleaming off the Dominie's silver wings. The plane felt very small and vulnerable as it nosed its way farther and farther from civilization.

Despite herself, Dawn began to relax. Three whole weeks on a tropical island. A house to herself, nobody fussing around her needing her gratitude. When you were sick it was lonely and crowded all at once. But she had escaped! Her parents could not make her crazy over here. There would be no more aggravating conversations about disabled athletes. She was thousands of miles from home and could do any damned thing she liked.

She felt like laughing hysterically. Instead she frowned at her heightened elation. It was the drugs, of course. They tended to distort her judgment. In the hospital she'd had morphine, and as far as Dawn was concerned the drip never flowed fast enough. Once she was off morphine, there was the refined cruelty of slow release Voltaren or OxyContin. To compensate, you had to take Percocet or Ibuprofen every few hours.

In the hospital, Dawn had quickly become a slave to the pill trolley. These days, she mixed her own cocktails. You had to be careful. Voltaren was stomach-ulcer territory. One a day was the limit. More than that and you spat blood. Sometimes Dawn didn't care and popped an extra anyway. But mostly she got by on Ibuprofen top-ups.

Lately she'd promised herself she would cut back. She didn't have the willpower to go cold turkey, but she was stretching the hours between doses. It was the best she could do. When you had constant pain, all you could think about was stopping it.

Next to her, Cody was hanging over the pilot's seat, deep in conversation with Annabel. Dawn caught snatches—Bevan had done Shuttleworth, some big plane museum in England. Annabel's mother was coming to stay. *Her mother!* What must she think of Annabel's lifestyle? Dawn felt sorry for the poor woman.

Shifting in her seat, she wriggled her toes to keep her circulation moving, weariness overtaking her once more. Her head ached from the uneven drone of the propellers and the acrid stench of petrol fumes. A dull vibration grinding along her legs reminded her that her pills were only thinly disguising the reality of her pain. What had she been thinking to come here? A mature person would have pulled herself together by now. Dawn was one of the lucky ones, after all. Other people had their spines destroyed and become paraplegic. What right did she have to feel sorry for herself? Why couldn't she just get on with living her life?

Tears stung. Dawn wiped them on her knuckles. For a moment, her eyes were drawn to her hands. They had been pretty before the accident, fine-boned and soft-skinned. Now they were covered in scars. Gingerly she touched the tender new skin, and looked up straight into Cody Stanton's searching eyes.

"Are you all right?" Cody sounded concerned.

If anyone asked her that again, she'd scream. Why couldn't people just mind their own business? "Of course I'm all right," she retorted.

For a moment Cody studied her, then with a small defeated shrug she turned away.

"Passion Bay to your right, folks," Annabel announced.

Dawn told herself she couldn't give a damn. But she peered down anyway, taking in the white beach, the dense green of the jungle, the unmistakable shape of Villa Luna with its wide front lawn and courtyard garden laid out like a brightly patterned handkerchief in the center. "I hope you know how to land this bloody crate," she grumbled as they dropped toward the treetops.

Annabel swooped low over the landing strip, then suddenly, jarringly, wound on full throttle. They shot straight up into the clouds, climbing giddily while Dawn squealed ineffectual protests from the back seat. Seconds later the world turned upside down and the tiny plane seemed to fall out of the sky.

"What the hell are you doing?" Dawn shrieked. "Are you trying to fucking kill us?"

Annabel did not answer until they had landed and the motors were finally silenced. Turning in her seat to face Dawn, she said in her polished drawl, "I thought I'd see if this bloody crate could manage a roll or two before we made our crash landing." Her expression was cool and unsympathetic. "Oh, and if you're planning to throw up, would you mind doing it outside? I'd hate to ruin my outfit cleaning up after you."

"YOU WERE A bit hard on her, sweetheart," Cody said later that evening. "I mean, she's obviously had a terrible accident."

Annabel glanced up from a folder she was leafing through. "Am I hearing this correctly? Are you really defending the dreadful Dawn?"

"She's not that bad," Cody objected. "She's just immature."

"You said that last time she was here, and that was nearly three years ago. When will the excuses run out? When she's retired, maybe? Or does walking with a cane exonerate one from common good manners?"

"You could have got us all killed."

"Now when would I risk your ass, let alone my own?" Annabel smiled sweetly.

Cody tossed a cushion at her. "I've died a thousand deaths in that plane, and you know it. Anyway, it wasn't such a bad idea of Dawn's."

"What idea?"

"Buying a new plane. The Dominie's over fifty years old. Can't we just put it in a museum and get a Lear or something?"

"Maybe we could, if we wanted to accept this." Annabel tossed the folder she had been holding across to Cody. "Read it and weep."

Cody admired the leather binding. "What is it?"

"Five million dollars in cash, plus another ten or so in shares. Someone wants to buy Moon Island."

Cody's brow furrowed as she thumbed through the pages of legalese. "Who?"

"Argus Chemco," Annabel supplied. "Some big multinational chemicals conglomerate. I'm meeting Robert Hausmann, their CEO, in Avarua later this week to discuss the offer. Evidently they're planning to expand their South Pacific operations and they want to establish a base in the Cook Islands."

"But Moon Island is miles from anywhere. It seems like a lot of money to pay for an office no one can find. Why don't they just buy New Zealand?"

Annabel smiled lightly. "Good point. Anyway I phoned Hausmann and told him he's wasting his time. But the guy still wants to make his pitch."

"Well, it's a free lunch. Maybe you should hear him out."

"You're not serious, are you?" Annabel frowned. "Do you want us to sell?"

"Good Lord, no," Cody said emphatically.

"You had me worried for a moment."

"I love it here. We live in paradise." Cody tossed the portfolio aside. "A Lear might have been fun, that's all."

"What can I say, sweetheart." Annabel reached for Cody. "Apart from anything else the airstrip's too short for a serious plane."

Cody heaved a protected sigh. "We could always land it on Raro and run a chopper for transport to the island."

Annabel's tone was incredulous. "Honey, I am not flying some celebrity ego-crutch across the Pacific. Not even for you. Is this some kind of mid-life crisis?" Cody stifled a giggle. Annabel was taking her seriously. "I know we're stuck out here in the tropics," she continued, "But if you really want a new toy, I guess we could get a Harley."

Cody heaved a sigh. "It wouldn't be the same without paved roads."

Annabel laughed. "You're just going to have to come to terms with slumming it on white beaches and getting cheap thrills at the expense of brats like Dawn Beaumont. It could be worse."

Burrowing into her, Cody slid a knee between her thighs. "You know, speaking of toys, we could get that Zodiac for the cruiser."

"Mmnhmn." Annabel rocked forward slightly, her mouth brushing Cody's. "Persuade me," she said.

# Chapter
# Three

"SO YOU'RE NOT dead after all." The voice came from the same direction as a stream of irreverent morning light. Camille Marquez was sitting at a small breakfast table calmly squeezing lemon into two cups of tea. Immaculate in raw silk pants, butter yellow shirt, thick gold bracelets, she gave a deceptively cool smile.

Head splitting, Grace elbowed herself upright, taking in the clothing strewn across the floor, the used smell of the bed linen, Camille's latex dams clinging to the bedspread. Her teeth felt furry. Rubbing her eyes, she caught the unmistakable scent of woman on her hands.

"So..." She tried for a kind of cocky nonchalance. The morning after was not her strong suit. "We... er..."

"We did." Camille crossed the room, handing Grace a cup of tea. "You weren't bad."

"Well, thanks." Grace choked on her first sip, images flitting across her mind—Camille laughing, the two of them sliding hot and naked amidst a tangle of sheets.

"You might have performed better if you weren't drunk," Camille put things right into perspective.

Grace deposited her tea on the bedside table and tenderly massaged her temples. Evidently she'd made the Big Impression. "I'm not usually such a slob," she said, wondering if she'd fallen asleep or something.

"And I'm not usually such a bitch." Camille indicated a neatly folded pile on the dressing table. "I got some fresh clothes for you. Take a shower, and we can get breakfast before you catch your plane." She checked her watch. "I'm going out now to send some faxes. I'll be about fifteen minutes."

Time management. The woman was obviously a formidable exponent of it. You had to be, Grace supposed, if you were organizing someone else's life as well as your own. Easing her legs off the bed, she forced herself woozily to her feet.

Camille was sorting papers into files. Glancing at Grace, she remarked, "Great body. Are you always so free with it?"

Grace frowned. Was she being called a slut now? "Only with kindred spirits," she returned tightly.

That earned a laugh. "You think I sleep with just anyone?" Camille snapped shut her leather briefcase. "I felt like good sex and I thought you could probably deliver."

"I'm flattered." Grace was at a loss for words. Apparently Camille orchestrated her sex life as methodically as her work.

Right now she was looking Grace up and down like a used-car salesman contemplating a low dollar trade-in. "You fuck around a lot, don't you, Grace?" she said. "Is that why you avoid having orgasms? You like to stay detached?"

Heat seeped into Grace's cheeks. Before she could prevent herself, she'd folded her arms defensively across her body. "I enjoy myself. Sex doesn't have to be orgasm-centric, surely?"

"Whatever." Camille shrugged, collected her briefcase and started toward the door. "So if it doesn't matter, how come you take care of yourself afterwards?"

The door clicked resolutely behind her and Grace flopped back onto the bed. "Well, fuck you too, Camille," she muttered.

SEVERAL DAYS LATER Annabel Worth strolled into the cool of the Rarotonga Resort Hotel lobby. She was right on time. When you get a note from the Cook Islands Premier insisting you meet some big shot on "a matter of importance to the Cook Islands," you turn up. She had even dressed for the occasion, wearing the kind of outfit she might have power-lunched in back home in Boston a thousand light-years ago.

Here on Rarotonga, a pink Chanel suit was guaranteed to fetch a few boggling stares from locals who seldom saw the owner of Moon Island in anything but chinos and a straw hat. Removing her sunglasses, Annabel checked her French plait and crossed the parquet tiles to the bar.

A man rose as she approached. He was sandy-haired, considerably shorter than she, and somewhere in his late forties. Like her, he was formally dressed, his suit and tie making no concession to the tropical surroundings.

"Ms. Worth?" At Annabel's brief nod, he extended his hand. "Robert B. Hausmann. Pleased to meet you."

Ushering her into a chair, he signaled a waiter. With slight puzzlement, Annabel observed him as he ordered their drinks. Robert B. Hausmann? The name seemed familiar. No doubt she had encountered it somewhere in the financial circles she'd once occupied.

"You're from back East, Mr. Hausmann?" she opened politely.

"New York." Annabel wondered about his accent. Highly educated, but rough edges. "Bronx and proud of it." He confirmed her suspicions. "And you? Boston?" This was said with the self-satisfaction of a man who knew he was right on the button.

Nodding, Annabel contained a smile. She recognized Hausmann's type—a short man with something to prove.

"Beautiful city, Boston," he remarked expansively. "Nearly lived there once." His tone suggested Boston's loss was greater than his. "Have you settled in these parts now, Ms. Worth?"

"I spend most of my time here. Although I do keep an apartment back home."

This caught his interest. "You have family in Boston?"

"That's right."

His eyes narrowed. Then, with a snap of the fingers, he declared, "Theo Worth. You're his daughter?"

Annabel tensed slightly. "You know my father?"

The response was enthusiastic. Robert B. Hausmann sometimes golfed with her father. He waxed lyrical over her parent's game, then asked her about the greens on Rarotonga.

"I'm afraid I wouldn't know. I've never shared my father's passion for golf."

Her companion waved an apologetic hand. "Then I bore you, I'm sorry." Leaning back in his chair, he surveyed her with a calculating expression. "So, what are your passions, Ms. Worth?" He flashed a set of perfectly even teeth and Annabel wondered whether she'd taken an instant dislike to him because he reminded her of a politician or because he wore too much expensive aftershave.

Their drinks arrived, and she sipped her mineral water. "I'm sure we're not here to talk about our passions, Mr. Hausmann," she said, keeping her polite smile in place.

"No, indeed." His glance slid past her breasts as if by accident. "I'll come straight to the point. As you know, we want this deal."

He expanded briskly. Argus Chemco was planning a major expansion of its Pacific Basin operations. This meant new offices around the region, employment growth, and millions of dollars in foreign currency earnings. It was very exciting...he was personally very excited.

The Pacific Basin was a growth marketplace for Argus. The next decade would be a boom time as Southeast Asia threw off the shackles of Third World poverty and embraced the consumerism that had made America great.

Annabel stemmed his flow. "So what exactly does Moon Island have to do with this vision, Mr. Hausmann?"

"I'll be frank, Annabel...may I call you Annabel?" He treated her to another brochure-perfect smile, confiding, "I have a feeling we're going to get to know each other very well." He had the good sense not to pat her knee, but Annabel guessed it was a close thing. "You've read the offer. Is there anything else I can tell you?"

As Annabel shook her head, he produced another leather-bound portfolio from his briefcase and extended it to her. "Excellent. This is the sale contract. As you will see, I have already signed."

Annabel placed the folder unopened on the table in front of her. She had finally caught on to his identity. Robert B. Hausmann had surfaced during the corporate raids and leveraged buyouts of the Eighties. Considered something of a wonder boy, he had touted his CEO skills around the business underbelly of New York, selling himself to the highest bidder, then generally orchestrating a takeover of his new employers by some shark who would offer him an even bigger package.

Argus had done just that, absorbing, under Hausmann's initiatives, the rival company he headed, only to find that he promptly deposed their own Chief Executive in a coup that had scandalized Wall Street. Led by Hausmann, Argus had flourished, swallowing competitors, scaling the Fortune 500 list and paying out unprecedented returns on its stock. So who was complaining?

Robert B. Hausmann embodied everything Annabel detested most about the world she'd left behind. He was spawned by, and promulgated, a value system that routinely destroyed viable companies, chopping up their assets and selling out their employees for the sake of fat fees for a greedy few at the top. As if that weren't enough, Annabel was sure she had read somewhere that an Argus subsidiary was under investigation for transporting dangerous chemical waste across the border to Mexico. It seemed Argus saw toxic waste management as a growth area and was rapidly expanding its global market share.

Frowning as she tried to recall the details, she said, "What exactly is the main focus of your operations, Mr. Hausmann?"

"Industrial chemicals. We fabricate, distribute and manage. As you will appreciate, most of our activities are commercially sensitive, and I'm not at liberty to go into detail about our development plans. Suffice to say we would propose a substantial facility for Moon Island."

"Doesn't sound like good news for the Cook Islands environment."

"On the contrary," Hausmann said. "Should Argus invest, as part of our corporate commitment, we will fund a brand new marine preservation unit based in Avarua. I'm thinking a dolphinarium for the tourists, plus a state of the art research center."

Argus must really want the deal bad, if they were willing to throw corporate bullion at the kind of image-building concept normally associated with morally bankrupt oil companies. The thought made Annabel uneasy.

"Our offer is very generous," he summarized in a self-congratulatory tone. "I think you'll agree that the combination of cash and stock is highly advantageous. I'm sure I don't need to emphasize the growth we are anticipating in the medium term. The offer is worth around fifteen million at today's values, but considerably more in the future if you hold the stock." He paused, perhaps to add weight to his words. "We both know that in some ways private wealth is a secondary consideration here, Annabel. I'm talking about the economy of these islands."

The gall of the man. He had read her like a book. Annabel even found herself momentarily swayed. The Cook Islands were desperate for foreign investment. The locals needed jobs and the government needed tax revenues. What right did she, a wealthy foreign resident, have to stand in the way of what could be an economic godsend? An ethical person would set her own selfish interests to one side.

"I've spoken at length with the Premier, and he has assured me of his personal commitment to the project." Hausmann drove home his advantage. "I know you'll feel the same way when you consider what this could mean to the local people."

Big finish. Soft-spoken Hausmann was a real carpetbagger. "I appreciate your interest," Annabel said more calmly than she felt. "But I have no plans to sell the island. It's my home."

Steely eyes gleamed knowingly across the table at her. Hausmann was in his element. This was his game. No one said yes to an initial offer, and he wouldn't have it any other way. He'd shown her the color of his money and now it was her job to feign disinterest and force him higher.

For a moment, Annabel was tempted to play chicken, but she held herself firmly in check. What did she have to prove to a man like Hausmann? She had left that world behind three years ago when she inherited Moon Island. She cared about the local people, and this man thought he could manipulate her on that basis. But it would take more than paternalistic lip-service to convince Annabel that a huge multi-national actually gave a damn about a bunch of islanders and their environment.

Resolutely, she slid the leather folder back across the table. "There's no point in continuing this discussion. Moon Island is not for sale."

Hausmann grinned, shark-like. "Everything is for sale, Annabel. You and I both know that."

"Perhaps where you come from," she said with a trace of bitterness.

He shrugged. "Take it. Read the fine print. That's all I ask. If you won't change your mind, I can accept that. I'm a reasonable man."

Rising, Annabel gathered up the folder and forced herself to shake his outstretched hand. "Very well, Mr. Hausmann. I'll read it. But my answer won't change. I'm not selling the island and that's final."

# Chapter
# Four

WHEN SHE FINALLY reached the southern end of the Hibiscus Bay, Dawn collapsed beneath a group of palm trees. Her legs throbbed, especially below her left knee where the messiest fracture had occurred. Protruding thin and naked from her shorts, her once powerful thighs scarcely seemed to belong to her. The muscles had wasted and her skin was mottled and faintly yellowish, the legacy of massive bruising. Long, angry scars ran like zippers down each limb. The surrounding flesh felt numb and dead.

Determined not to cry, Dawn propped herself against a husky palm trunk and took a long, grateful swig from her water flask. She was screwing the top on when a voice nearby inquired, "May I have a sip of that?"

With a start of fright, Dawn craned around. A woman emerged from behind the next palm tree. She was tall and slim, with the kind of fine, straight coppery hair usually associated with pale skin and freckles. Only this woman was very tanned. Surveying Dawn with eyes that also seemed too dark for her coloring, she said, "I'm sorry, did I frighten you?

"It's okay." Avoiding her piercing gaze, Dawn mechanically handed over the flask and watched the stranger drink.

She wore cotton drill shorts, slouch hat, and a white shirt with the sleeves rolled up. Over this was a loose khaki vest, its many pockets bulging with mysterious contents. The outfit seemed an odd choice for a day at the beach.

Perhaps realizing how out of place she looked, the woman produced a slightly lopsided smile as she returned the flask. "I'm Grace Ramsay. And in case you're wondering, I'm here working." Her voice was low and slightly English-sounding.

Dawn wished there were some way of avoiding the formality of exchanging names. God only knew where it would lead. The woman was probably staying somewhere nearby. Maybe she would expect to form one of those sordid holiday friendships where people confide all sorts of intimate information, knowing that they'll never see each other again. Dawn needed that like a redback in her bra. But noting the stranger's expectant expression, she mumbled resignedly, "I'm Dawn Beaumont."

"You're Australian?"

"I'm from Sydney."

"Are you staying around here?" That candid gaze moved slowly over her body, halting at her legs.

Dawn felt as if she'd just been touched instead of looked at. Blushing, she reached for her cane. What a dumb question. Of course she was staying here. Why else would she be wandering along the beach on some desert island miles from civilization?

Something of her scorn must have showed, because the copper-haired woman gave another of those lopsided grins. "Blinding glimpse of the obvious, huh?"

Her smile was so engaging that Dawn returned it despite herself. "I'm staying over there," she said, pointing back along the bay. "In Frangipani Cottage."

"Really? You're my neighbor then. I'm only five minutes' walk from you."

"Great," Dawn said flatly. At least now she knew which track to avoid. She had come to this place for peace and quiet. That did not include making meaningless chitchat with inquisitive strangers. Conscious of Grace Ramsay's scrutiny, she pulled herself clumsily to her feet and, leaning on her stick, brushed the sand off her shorts. Grace was not as tall as Dawn had first thought. Her straight, athletic posture simply gave that impression.

From behind the safety of her shades, Dawn examined the stranger more closely. She really was quite striking, and she looked like the type who knew it, too. There was something about her—an unnerving self-awareness. It was then that she noticed a diamond stud beaming expensive light from one of Grace's earlobes.

As Dawn gazed, Grace lifted a hand to toy with the diamond earring. "You're welcome to drop in some time for coffee."

Dawn's stomach chose that moment to pitch sharply, and she lifted accusing eyes to the sun. She was feeling breathless and light-headed. Maybe she'd taken too many painkillers that morning. Shifting the weight off her heels, she tried to remember. One Voltaren and four Ibuprofen. Definitely time to cut down. Perspiration gathered around her nose and forehead. She slid a hand inside the rim of her hat to wipe it away.

Grace Ramsay's eyes narrowed slightly at the gesture. "Are you all right?"

"I'm fine, thank you," Dawn replied stiffly. The woman was giving her the jitters. Strangers often had that effect these days. It took such an effort to make them feel comfortable.

"I could walk you home if you like," Grace offered.

Dawn took a quick pace back, shaking her head. "I'm okay. Honestly."

"If you say so." Something in those charcoal eyes, a detached amusement, irritated Dawn—"Well, I'll be seeing you then," Grace added, still leaning casually against the tree trunk. "Soon, I hope."


RELIEVED TO BE by herself once more, Dawn limped along the water line. *Soon, I hope.* What did the woman mean by that? Was she planning a neighborly visit? Dawn hoped not. Dismissing the conversation from her mind, she glanced apprehensively over her shoulder. The beach was deserted. It would have been easy to imagine she was the only person on the whole island. Heaving a pent-up sigh, she flopped onto the sand and pulled off her sweaty shorts and top.

Her skin tingled pleasantly as the sun dried the moisture from its surface. Dawn opened her beach bag and subjected her bikini to a cursory inspection. She should put it on, she supposed, but swimming naked was one of the few things she had enjoyed about her last stay on Moon Island. There were nude beaches in Australia, of course, but parading about in front of an audience was not her idea of a good time.

Occasionally Dawn felt dismayed at her self-consciousness. It was crazy for a swimmer to have a hang-up about showing off her body. When she was training, she virtually lived in a swimsuit, but that was different somehow.

At the beach men were such pervs, even the decent ones. If you wanted to be left alone, you had to swim at Tamarama, the gay beach where the men were all busy ogling one another. And, of course, there was always this place with its bizarre women-only rules.

Flexing her ruined legs, Dawn was aware of a guilty relief that men were banned from Moon Island. She would be able to wear shorts the whole time she was here. Or nothing at all. Confirming her solitude with another quick glance along the beach, she returned her bikini to her bag and set about plaiting her hair into a thick braid. It sat hot and heavy on her neck, and for a split second Dawn imagined it gone, cut boyishly short like that woman Grace's. That was a ridiculous idea, she decided almost as soon as she contemplated it. She'd had long hair ever since she could remember. It suited her. Besides, guys liked it.

Dawn clambered to her feet and dropped her stick on top of her clothes. It was strange walking without it, like balancing on a wall, scared to look down in case she fell. Trying not to feel insecure, she forced her eyes off her feet and proceeded along the beach in a cautious gait.

Hibiscus Bay was exactly as she had always imagined Robinson Crusoe's beach might be: timeless, exotic, impossibly tranquil. The sand beneath her feet was hot and yielding. Out beyond the lagoon, a coral reef shimmered like a pink mirage beneath the surface.

Dawn waded into the sea until she was buoyed off her feet. Drifting a few yards with the gentle current, she rolled onto her back, closed her eyes, and lost herself in the hollow glub of bubbles rising. The water was warm and soothing. With a small murmur of contentment, she rested her hands on her belly. Despite the lack of exercise, she was still flat and firm. Experimentally, she cupped her breasts. They were slightly smaller than usual— she'd lost a lot of weight since the accident. In fact, her whole body felt light and brittle.

Dawn had never realized how much she took her physical strength for granted until it was taken from her. It was scary to feel so fragile. She guessed her mother's force-feeding regime was a response to the dramatic change. She'd been living at home ever since she got out of the hospital. What a nightmare. Her parents just didn't seem to realize that she wasn't thirteen any more. She no longer had to go to church or have the lights out at nine o'clock. They lived in a shrine of cups, ribbons and newspaper cuttings of their champion daughter. One reporter had been so confused by the way they talked about her, he thought she must be dead.

Thank God her mother wasn't here, Dawn thought, and kicked out tentatively. It was not the first time she'd swum since the accident. Once the plaster was off, her physiotherapy had involved daily exercise in a pool. She'd done routines in a group, everyone grunting and complaining. Down at the other end of the pool were the paraplegics—just in case her own group thought they had problems.

Initially Dawn had been thrilled when she finally finished the hospital program. All those maimed bodies, people staggering along on artificial limbs, the constant cries of pain and frustration. Who needed it? Yet she missed her particular group of friends. In the orthopedic ward, they had been in adjoining beds, and with nothing better to do than eat, sleep, read, and watch the soaps, they had spent most of their time talking.

There was Delia, the secretary whose woman boss sent her flowers twice a week and paid the singing telegram people to come and cheer her up. Monique with the three kids and the slob of a husband she wanted to leave. Jane whose fiancé came every day after work with chocolates, then ate them himself because she was on a diet.

Dawn had never talked so much with other women in her entire life. It was different without men around. They could discuss anything they liked: sex, politics, their families. She had started to view those women as her only real friends, the only people who understood what she was going through.

Immediately after the accident, she'd had numerous visitors, of course. But once the novelty wore off, only her parents and Trish came regularly. Everyone else had their own lives to lead, Dawn reasoned. Yet it hurt to read about things her former teammates did and to realize she hadn't seen any of them in months.

There was no point dwelling on it, Dawn reminded herself and began an idle over-arm, pausing occasionally to mark herself against the bright shape of her towel. To her surprise, she swam the entire length of the bay, picking up speed as she got into her stroke. She was almost reluctant to stop, but common sense dictated that she slow down while she was still strong enough to swim ashore.

Feeling ridiculously proud of herself, she switched to a modest breaststroke, only to have her delight quickly fade. Her legs generated virtually no push at all. She couldn't even get them in time with each other. Overwhelmed with dismay, she shook the water from her eyes and flipped onto her back, allowing the sea to cradle her.

Guilt and bitterness consumed her. It really was true. She had crashed that car, killed her teammate, and destroyed her own swimming career, all for the sake of a few drinks with Nigel Myers. Tears merged with the salt water washing her temples, and she blinked up at the empty sky. How could one dumb choice have destroyed so much? She was fortunate she had not been prosecuted on a DWI rap. Her blood alcohol had been just under the limit.

Eventually something brushed her back and she connected gently with sand. For a few long moments, she succumbed to the balmy caresses of the breaking tide, then she got to her feet and looked around for her towel.

It was way down the beach. Served her right for getting distracted, she thought wryly. She managed to limp a few paces toward it when she was gripped by the same curious light-headedness she'd experienced earlier talking to that copper-haired woman. Shaking her head, she proceeded more slowly. It was no good. Her legs felt like cooked spaghetti.

Miserably conscious of her clammy skin, Dawn drew a shallow breath. Why hadn't she listened to Cody and Annabel's warnings about the sun? Why was she always so pig-headed? Head spinning, she ventured another a small step. The sand swayed and undulated in front of her. Blood rushed in her ears. Overhead, gulls lamented. Dawn stared up at them, watching a bird soar higher and higher. Her eyes closed against the impossible brightness of the sun, and she didn't even feel her face hit the sand.

DAWN HAD NO idea how much time had passed when she blinked up into a dark, concerned stare.

"I'm going to get you into some shade," Grace Ramsay said in her low clipped way. "Put your arms around my neck."

Dawn hesitated, but the arm supporting her shoulders had already tightened and another slid beneath her knees. "It's okay"—that teasing smile—"I won't drop you."

Dawn felt so weak she could only rest her head against Grace's shoulder. There was something comforting about being cradled that way, immersed in a mixture of scents—salt, skin, sun on cotton, some kind of spicy perfume. A hint of cloves.

At the edge of the jungle, Grace lowered Dawn onto the sandy earth, commenting, "I think you've had too much sun." Her arm was still loosely around Dawn's waist and her face was very close. It was an interesting face, not beautiful, but arresting. Probably the eyes, Dawn decided. Thickly fringed with long straight black eyelashes, they were the color of wet graphite. Tiny emerald flecks made the color shift.

Dawn stared. She couldn't help herself.

Grace stared back, eyes wickedly appreciative. "I see you're a natural blonde," she said in a husky purr.

Dawn's cheeks burned. She was completely naked, she remembered. And Grace Ramsay was looking her up and down, calm as you please. Mortified, Dawn wriggled upright. Her limbs felt glutinous. "Please," she stammered, "get my clothes."

An infuriating grin twitched the corners of Grace's mouth, but she rose obediently and sauntered across the sand to collect the discarded bag.

Dawn could hardly believe her eyes. It was that walk. The one she hated. The calm swagger she associated irrevocably with Cody Stanton. When Grace returned, Dawn raised an arm to cover her breasts.

The protective gesture only seemed to amuse her companion. "Don't let it bother you, Dawn." With insolent self-assurance, Grace added, "I've seen it all before."

What was that supposed to mean? Lobbing her most withering look at the stranger, Dawn dragged on her clothes and knotted her belt with shaking fingers. She didn't like Grace Ramsay, she decided. Something about her attitude bugged the hell out of Dawn.

Seemingly impervious, Grace said, "I think I'd better walk you home."

"That won't be necessary," Dawn snapped.

Grace looked unmoved. "That's what you thought last time. So I'm going to tag along just in case. Can you walk? Or would you like me to carry you?"

Vehemently Dawn shook her head. "I said I can manage. See?" She scrambled to feet to prove it. "I'm perfectly all right."

Grace's eyes flickered with growing impatience. "Are you always so defensive about your disability, Dawn?" she drawled. "Or have you just taken a particular dislike to me?"

Dawn studied her feet. She was being rude and unreasonable, she supposed. It was no way to treat a stranger whose worst crime was trying to help her. If she had any sense, she would accept Grace's offer and be thankful. Ashamed, she wriggled her toes, noticing the chipped crimson polish. Too bad, she thought recklessly. Once upon a time she was very picky about personal grooming, but she didn't have to impress anyone anymore.

She lifted reluctant eyes. "I'm sorry I snapped at you," she managed. "I just—I'm not feeling very well."

Grace subjected her to a cool, measuring stare. "We're all entitled to an off day." Then she smiled, all charm and nonchalance.

# Chapter
# Five

IT TOOK FAR too long to reach Frangipani Cottage. The path through the jungle was well trodden but narrow, and the effort of pushing aside the thickly interwoven creepers tired Dawn quickly. Watching Grace stroll ahead of her, she wondered what it was about the woman that got under her skin.

Dawn guessed she was about thirty. At a glance she looked younger, somehow boyish. It was a fashionable look, the short hair, long legs, distinct shoulder muscles. Dawn's eyes were drawn to the neat roll of her hips and she found herself thinking about Cody Stanton again. Grace had the same kind of streetwise air about her. Dawn recalled a conversation she'd had with one of the women staying on the island the last time she was here. Sexy. That was what she'd called Cody.

Bothered, she forced her eyes off the woman in front of her. Maybe they'd gone to the same deportment classes. Or maybe...she fled from the idea. She didn't want to think about the fact that Cody Stanton was a lesbian.

They were nearing Frangipani Cottage. It was set on a slight rise on the northeastern face of the island. Before the hurricane three years ago, it had been the only dwelling on this part of the island and was surrounded by old frangipani and gardenia trees. Hurricane Mary and its attendant tsunami had devastated both house and gardens, leaving a trail of uprooted foliage and a mere shell where the cottage had stood.

The new cottage was built farther back from the ocean for protection from the tidal waves that had claimed its predecessor. A second cottage had been constructed at the same time, even farther inland.

In the fecundity of the tropics, the new gardens had quickly erased all evidence of Hurricane Mary. Looking at Frangipani Cottage now, it was difficult to imagine any other landscape. Lush greenery surrounded the place, teeming with insects and bird life, bougainvillea meandered across the verandah, and everything smelled green and moist.

Halting at the verandah, Grace propped herself against a wooden pillar, removing her hat to fan her face indolently. Her hair, bright in the afternoon sun, feathered damply over her forehead. With a combination of guilt and annoyance, Dawn dragged herself up the whitewashed steps. Now that they were here, the least she could do was offer her visitor a glass of water or something.

Catching a hint of challenge in Grace's expression, she grudgingly invited her in, adding, "Would you like a cup of tea?" Maybe Grace had other plans.

Apparently not. In the kitchen she removed her vest and suspended it casually over the back of a chair. The movement parted her white shirt where it was unbuttoned, and Dawn caught a glimpse of tanned breast and dark nipple. Hastily she turned to the little gas stove, and after several futile attempts, managed to light the burner. Grace Ramsay went without a bra. So what? This was Moon Island. There was no one to see. Except women.

Dawn deposited a couple of mugs on the table. She was absurdly conscious of Grace's bold eyes tracing her every movement. Was the woman trying to make her nervous?

"You're here alone?" Grace asked in a conversational tone.

Dawn mumbled a yes. The kettle still wasn't boiling. She fidgeted beside the stove.

"Me, too," Grace said. "It's a great place to come for some time out. How long are you staying?"

"Three weeks," Dawn responded.

"So am I." Grace glanced wryly at her vest. "I wish I had more free time to enjoy the place."

Determined to avoid drawing out the visit, Dawn refrained from asking what exactly Grace did. Once this was over, she would have made her concession to good manners. She wouldn't need to see her neighbor again. To her relief the water was finally boiling. She slopped it carelessly into a teapot.

"What part of Sydney are you from?" Grace asked.

"My family lives in Randwick."

"I worked in Sydney a few years back." When Dawn did not respond, Grace volunteered, "I'm a scientist." Her tone was matter-of-fact, as though there was nothing at all unusual in this revelation, as though a woman scientist was as commonplace and unspectacular as a nurse or a receptionist.

Dawn felt slightly piqued, but curious, too. "Is that what you're doing here on the island—something scientific?"

"You could say that." Grace's eyes were guarded all of a sudden. "I'm writing a report on coral reef structures in the

South Pacific." She went on to describe some research project she was involved in. None of the technical terms made any sense to Dawn.

"It sounds fascinating," Dawn lied.

"I'm enjoying it." Grace gave a teasing smile, as if she knew Dawn found the very idea boring and incomprehensible. "I'm usually based in New York, but I get to travel all over."

"Who do you work for?"

Again the hesitation. "I'm a consultant. I work on contract, usually for big international companies."

She sounded uncomfortable. Perhaps she was embarrassed about being so successful, Dawn conjectured. Grace was obviously one of those tough, clever women who negotiated highly paid assignments for themselves all over the world. She wasn't stuck in the suburbs minding kids for a bunch of Westies while they went to their boring jobs.

Dawn glanced at Grace's hands. They were finely boned, the fingers long and graceful in their movements. No wedding ring; not even the telltale mark of one recently discarded. Obviously Grace didn't have a man to wait on when she got home. She probably lived alone in some big impractical apartment with cream-colored everything. She probably ate out for every meal. She probably owned her own sports car...

Swallowing a sigh, Dawn got a grip on herself. What did she care how Grace Ramsay lived?

Grace got to her feet, and again Dawn noticed the way her shirt dragged across her small high breasts, compressing her dark nipples against the fabric. She took in the firm athletic muscling of her shoulders and arms, then wished she wasn't so fascinated by the sight. What on earth was the matter with her? Was she noticing other women's bodies all of a sudden because hers was ruined?

Exhausted suddenly, Dawn stifled a yawn and followed Grace out onto the verandah. They stood in silence, taking in the view across the jungle to the sea. The air was tinted with a spicy scent. Cloves. It was quite delicious. For a second Dawn wondered dreamily if it was some exotic plant in her garden, then she traced the source to Grace's shirt, remembering that smell as she was being carried, naked, along the beach.

"Well, thanks for the tea." Grace searched Dawn's face for a moment, as if seeking the answer to an unspoken question.

Bemused, Dawn managed a half-hearted smile. "Um...thanks for walking me home." It felt awkward, the two of them standing there on the verandah, being so polite.

Grace hesitated. "I'll be seeing you, Dawn." She touched

Dawn's arm for a fleeting second.

Warmth flooded Dawn's cheeks and her skin prickled under Grace's fingers. It was only after she'd watched Grace saunter into the jungle that she realized she had been holding her breath. Taking a sharp, shallow gulp of air, she retreated indoors and sought out her bed. A long time later, staring up at her ceiling, she was engulfed by a clamoring uneasiness. Would she see the overly friendly Grace Ramsay again? Not if she could help it.

IT WAS LATE afternoon when Dawn awoke from her nap. Drowsily, she rolled onto her back, swallowing the clean fragrant air and listening to the jumbled cacophony beyond her window. The jungle was never quiet. You could almost hear it growing. The sounds of pre-dusk were busy, chaotic, signaling the sun's impending demise. Insects chirped relentlessly, frogs croaked, and all over the island, creatures recovered from the heat of the day and bustled home, foraging for final tidbits on the way.

It was so different from the city. No horns blaring, traffic whining, radios, TVs, hordes of people. Just the ever-present pulse of the ocean and the comforting *sotto voce* of nature at work.

Dawn left her bed and wandered out to the kitchen, staring disconsolately at the two half-full mugs still sitting on the table. It would be sensible to make herself a meal. The tiny refrigerator was jammed with tempting foods. But she wasn't particularly hungry. Pouring a large glass of pineapple juice instead, she dragged herself out onto the verandah and flopped into a deep cane chair.

She could always read a book. She'd brought a pile of Jackie Collins paperbacks with her.

Or she could write a letter:

*Dear Nigel,*

*How is training coming along? Thank you for the flowers. I'm having a holiday in the Cook Islands. I'll phone you when I get back.*

Or would she? Nigel hadn't exactly broken records to sit at her bedside. What had she expected? They'd only dated a few times, yet somehow Nigel had meant more to her than any of the other men at the swimming club. He'd always given his mates the impression that there was something between them.

He was busy, of course. Olympic selection was only months away, and he could still improve his times. She was a sportswoman. She could understand that imperative. Knotting her fingers behind her head, she sought comfort in her exercise routine.

Lift, flex and stretch, flex and stretch.

The distraction tactic failed. She couldn't avoid thinking about the accident. Even now, six months later, it barely felt real. It had all happened so fast. Someone had offered her a ride home but she'd said no. She had her own car and besides, Nigel had asked her to stay for another drink. Two glasses later he was asking her to come home with him and Dawn was groping for an excuse to decline. She was taking Lynda, she'd said. Someone always had to drop Lynda off—she didn't drive.

Nigel had been surly. He had a right to be, she supposed. She had been saying no to him for months, and she wasn't even sure why. That night he had called her a frigid tease and one or two other insulting things, and she'd driven off in a rage. She hadn't even seen the corner. Even now she couldn't remember what had happened. One minute Lynda was asking her to slow down and the next Dawn woke up in a hospital bed, a drip in her arm and a nurse shining a torch in her eyes.

Dawn swallowed the lump in her throat and chewed at a couple of fingernails. There was no point in reliving the past. What's done is done, she told herself. Then she started to cry in earnest.

She was still sitting there, head in her hands, when a voice she dreaded inquired, "Dawn?"

Jerking upright, she met a pair of quizzical gray eyes. "Oh, it's you."

Cody Stanton took in her tear-stained face without comment. Uninvited, she occupied the other cane chair.

She looked so relaxed and happy that Dawn felt like hitting her. "Go away," she mumbled resentfully.

Unfazed, Cody stayed where she was. "Do you want to talk about it, Dawn?" She reached out and took one of Dawn's hands.

"No, I don't." Dawn snatched her hand away. "It's none of your business."

"Dawn," Cody persisted. "I might be able to help you if you'd let me." Moving her chair closer to Dawn's, she added quietly, "I know you and I have never gotten along. And I know you don't like me or approve of the way I live, but..."

Dawn looked at Cody. "That's not true," she whispered, conscious of color flooding her cheeks.

For a split second Cody's face registered surprise, then her expression relaxed into its usual easygoing charm. "Then how about coming back to Villa Luna with me now," she coaxed. "Annabel's making something yummy for dinner. We could get drunk and reminisce about hurricanes. Seriously, how bad could it be?"

Even as Dawn opened her mouth to decline, she found herself responding to Cody's enthusiasm with a small, watery smile.

Her visitor instantly read this as acceptance. "Great. Go get your stuff, and I'll wait for you out here."

Torn between irritation and gratitude, Dawn got to her feet. Once upon a time, she would have told Cody to go away, then sat around feeling sorry for herself for the rest of the night. But right now, she didn't feel like being a martyr. Vacillating for a moment, she said, "I hope you're not expecting me to walk."

It was worse than that.

Their transport was tethered beneath a palm tree and snorted as Cody tightened its saddle. Recognizing the black horse she had shared the cave with during the hurricane, Dawn nearly turned around and went straight back inside. The animal didn't like her back then. Why would now be any different? "I can't do this," she protested as Cody helped her into the saddle. "I don't know how to ride."

"No worries. I do." Cody swung up behind her and reached around, placing Dawn's hands firmly on a raised leather mound in front of her. "That's called the pommel. Just hang on to it and leave the rest to me and Kahlo."

Protesting volubly, Dawn made a grab for the saddle as they plunged into the jungle. They seemed awfully high up and the black horse was pulling at the reins and tossing its head like a wild animal.

"She's got some attitude, today," Cody commented, stretching past Dawn to pat the dark muscular neck.

"Terrific. Black Beauty runs amok." Dawn sat stiffly, trying to keep her distance from Cody—not easy when you're stuck two-up on a saddle. "I don't think she likes me."

"Relax." Cody was infuriatingly blasé. "You might even enjoy it. If she senses you're nervous, she'll give us a hard time."

With a groan, Dawn forced herself to relax, allowing the tension to seep from her muscles. The only problem with her new posture was how close it brought her to Cody. She was acutely conscious of the arms on either side of her, the press of Cody's thighs, her body warm and close.

Their semi-embrace felt both unnerving and soothing. Lulled by the swaying gait of the horse, Dawn allowed herself to drift, and for one appalling moment she felt herself sinking back against Cody, almost cradled. Abruptly, her mind leapt to the memory of Cody and Annabel kissing on Passion Bay and she jerked herself upright, a peculiar gnawing in the pit of her stomach.

"Are you comfortable?" Cody's breath grazed her cheek.

Mouth as dry as dust, Dawn nodded mutely. What on earth was the matter with her? With bizarre fascination, she stared at Cody's arms, at the hands controlling the reins. She was overcome by a powerful urge to touch her, stroke her, nestle against her. Disbelief clouded her consciousness like a swarm of wasps. She was attracted to Cody. No! It couldn't be true!

Hunching forward, she clutched the pommel with sweaty fingers. Of course it wasn't true. It was her imagination, probably the aftermath of sunstroke. And the drugs she took had some peculiar side effects. Dawn ordered herself to breathe, stay calm and think logically. She couldn't possibly be attracted to Cody. Cody was a woman. And not just a woman, she reminded herself hastily, a lesbian.

ANNABEL MET THEM on the verandah of Villa Luna. Wearing a sapphire blue sarong, she looked like a film star. Dawn fought off a stab of envy and hung back as Cody planted a kiss squarely on her lover's mouth before leading Kahlo off.

"I'm so glad you could come." Annabel greeted Dawn as if she were genuinely pleased to see her, a highly unlikely state of affairs. "I can't believe it's been nearly three years since you were here last."

Dawn managed a smile. "Neither can I."

Annabel showed her inside and Dawn sank into a chair. Watching Annabel pour their drinks, she tried not to think about her and Cody together, kissing and God knows what else.

Handing Dawn a glass, Annabel sat on the sofa opposite. She was wearing her platinum hair loose, and it spilled fine and silky across her pale shoulders. Dawn gazed at her curiously. Annabel was the only albino she'd ever seen close up. The whiteness of her hair and skin was astonishing. How on earth did she manage to avoid getting burnt, living out here on an island? It wasn't as if she stayed indoors all the time.

"Do you live here all year round?" Dawn asked, taking a prolonged drink and licking her lips with pleasure. The cocktail was wonderful, a mixture of coconut milk and tropical fruit juice.

"Almost," Annabel said. "We visit Cody's mother in New Zealand quite often, and we spend time at my place in Boston."

"Otherwise Annabel suffers shopping withdrawal," teased a voice from the doorway. Cody wandered into the room, poured herself a drink, and sat down beside Annabel, resting a casual hand on her knee.

Dawn tried not to be fascinated by the intimate gesture.

You'd think they could be more discreet instead of flaunting their relationship so blatantly. It was downright embarrassing. Lifting censorious eyes, she intercepted a look that passed between them, a look of such undiluted passion that her mouth went dry with shock. They were besotted with each other. Hopelessly in love. And it seemed so natural.

Dawn felt twitchy just thinking about it. Forcing her thoughts to Nigel, she tried to envision having feelings like that for him, for anyone. It was useless. She couldn't begin to imagine it. Maybe she was a shallow person. Maybe she would never experience true love, never share with anyone whatever it was that Cody and Annabel had. She probably wouldn't recognize the emotion if she fell over it.

Her attention was drawn again to the two women, and all of a sudden she found herself envying them bitterly, forgetting they weren't normal. They just looked so happy. Tears of self-pity stung her eyes. Dawn rubbed them impatiently aside and looked up to find Cody watching her.

"Dawn, what is it?"

"Nothing." She folded defensive arms across her stomach. "I'm just tired."

Annabel was staring too, those strange lavender eyes wide and concerned. "Was it the ride? You're looking quite ill."

"No. I'm fine. Really."

"Maybe you should lie down before dinner," Annabel said. "I'll get you an aspirin."

"No!" Dawn bit her lip. She hadn't meant to sound so hostile, but a terrible anger welled inside her. She wanted to smash her glass and scream at the world that there was no God because a God with any decency would never have done this to her.

Abruptly, she got to her feet and hobbled to the open window. She was cracking up, she thought with a surge of panic. They would put her on lithium, like one of the women in her hospital ward, and she would turn into a zombie. Lifting trembling fingers to her forehead, she stared out at the sunset. The sky was a shifting palette of orange, cerise, pink, and gold. Distracted by its astounding beauty, she took a few deep breaths, watching the procession of colors from sapphire through heliotrope to amethyst, until finally the blood-red sun fused with the ocean.

Conscious, then, of the other women, she said dully, "It's my legs. They hurt most of the time, and I'm trying to cut down on my painkillers."

A jumpy silence followed.

"Was it a car accident?" Cody asked eventually.

To Dawn's horror she felt tears streaming down her face, and her shoulders shook uncontrollably. "It's the worst thing that's ever happened to me," she cried harshly. "I wish I were dead!"

Cody crossed the room and gently took Dawn in her arms. For a long while, the two women stood there, Dawn sobbing and Cody rubbing her back and making soothing noises.

"I don't know what to do," Dawn wept. "I've lost everything. I'll never swim again. I was training for the Olympic trials. I just can't believe it." She wiped her face with her arm, mortified at breaking down in front of these women. Backing out of Cody's embrace, she sagged against the window frame. "Oh, what does it matter?" she said bleakly. "It's my problem, not yours."

"Dawn." Annabel approached, a box of tissues in her hand. "Please don't punish yourself for needing support."

Dawn took the box. The kindness in Annabel's voice only made her more upset. Annabel was being nice to her, after all the things she had thought about her and Cody. Paralyzed with shame, she looked up, caught the shimmer of tears in Annabel's eyes, and cried even harder. She barely noticed being led out onto the verandah and eased gently into a deep two-seater overlooking the ocean.

After a long silence, Annabel spoke. "Isn't it beautiful?" She gestured at the view across Passion Bay.

It was breathtaking. The moon hung in the night sky like a well-polished tin, staining the ocean quicksilver. The air was warm and sultry, scented with the crush of tropical leaves and flowers. "I remember this view." Dawn hiccupped. "I used to sit out here night after night when we were waiting to be rescued."

Back then, she had always thought she was just keeping watch for the steamer. But it was much more than that, she realized with a flash of understanding. Looking out across Passion Bay, you couldn't help but feel a sense of belonging, of being part of the miracle of life.

Annabel smiled contentedly. "I think this is my favorite place on earth. Whenever I'm away from here I feel like I'm serving a prison sentence. I just can't wait to get back." She laughed as though amused at herself. "And to think, I used to be such a city girl."

Meeting her eyes, Dawn noticed she was alone with Annabel. Where was Cody?

Annabel must have read her mind. "I've put Cody to work in the kitchen. Hopefully, any minute we'll be summoned to a delicious meal. I don't think she'll have time to burn it."

Dawn blew her nose. "I feel really stupid crying like this."

"Please don't. As far as I'm concerned you can cry all you want while you're with us."

"I've done enough crying for one lifetime." Dawn twisted her hands in her lap. "I need to get my act together and do something with my life. But I feel so... stuck. All I ever wanted was to swim."

"Surely that couldn't last forever. What were you planning to do once you retired?"

"I never really thought about it. I guess I had vague ideas about coaching. And I figured I'd get married someday, have kids. But—"

"But?" Annabel raised her eyebrows.

Dawn gave a harsh little laugh. "Well, look at me. I can't even walk properly. My legs look like they've been run over by a lawn mower and my hands, too. Who's going to marry me now?"

"A person with enough depth to look beyond a few scars," Annabel replied. "Are you seeing anyone at the moment?"

"Nobody special," Dawn responded gruffly, her thoughts straying to Nigel. "I mean, there was someone. But it wasn't serious."

Annabel's expression was cautious. "You're not seeing him anymore?"

Dawn studied her feet, unsure how to answer. She never really was seeing him, was she? "He's been busy." Knowing she sounded evasive, she paused to clear her throat. "He's a finalist for Olympic selection."

Annabel nodded as if she understood. She seemed about to say something else when Cody appeared with the news that dinner was served and that this time she hadn't burnt the sauce.


"DON'T STRAIGHT WOMEN have complicated lives?" Cody mumbled a long time later, snuggling into Annabel in the sleepy darkness.

Annabel kissed her cheek. "We all have our problems. Ours are not so very different from theirs."

"It sounds like he dumped her." Cody sighed disgustedly. "What a prince."

"She's pretending it doesn't matter," Annabel said. "But I don't think it's done much for her self-esteem."

"Well, that's the trouble with buying into men's beauty standards. You're stuffed unless you measure up."

"You know," Annabel mused, recalling an expression she had caught on Dawn's face more than once that evening, "I get the distinct impression that, underneath it all, Dawn's not that stuck on men."

Cody laughed. "You don't know the woman, sweetheart! You didn't have to spend forty-eight hours trapped in a cave with her. All she could talk about was men. And she's a raving homophobe."

"That doesn't mean anything. She could be latent."

Cody groaned. "Lesbian reality strikes again. Every woman is a dyke. Honestly, Annabel, you're straight out of the seventies sometimes."

Annabel prodded her playfully in the ribs. "Okay smart-ass. Then maybe you can explain how come Dawn has such a huge crush on you if she's so super-straight."

Cody stiffened. "What do you mean?"

"Observant, aren't we? Don't tell me you haven't noticed. She only stares at you all the time and blushes every time you speak to her."

"Straight woman often get jumpy around me," Cody said. "You don't get so much of that kind of thing because you look so..."

"So what?" Annabel made a grab for Cody as she tried to escape beneath the covers. "You were going to say safe, weren't you? Passing?"

"No, I wasn't." Cody fended her off. "I was going to say...pretty. Beautiful." Her arms slid around Annabel, and she lifted her hair to kiss the nape of her neck. "Absolutely ravishing."

"Don't think you can sweet-talk me." Annabel slapped her hands away. "You're evading the issue. Dawn Beaumont definitely has a crush on you."

Cody sighed dramatically. "You read too many romances."

"We'll see," Annabel murmured with prim conviction. She thought about Dawn recovering from a traumatic accident, emotionally vulnerable, and confused about her sexuality. It was a volatile combination. For a brief crazy second she panicked at what it might lead to. She hoped Cody would tread carefully. Otherwise they could be in for three very uncomfortable weeks.

# Chapter
## Six

GRACE AWOKE SWEATING and disoriented. Whitewashed walls surrounded her, sterile in the half-light. Drawn by the large open window above her bed, she slowly focused on the view it framed, listening for the sounds that anchored her to reality.

There was only stillness, the mystical calm that foretells the coming of dawn, that pause when every living creature seems to hold its breath before saluting the day. The eerie moment passed. A bird cried, a pale green streak of light traversed the sky, and a morning breeze stirred the ocean's face.

Tension dissolving, Grace pushed off her bedclothes and stretched. A peculiar image hovered in her consciousness—the face of an animal, a dog. She frowned. She had never owned a dog, only cats. One cat. Missy. She had died several years ago and Grace had decided not to have another pet.

She must have dreamed about the dog. How odd. Normally she never remembered anything about The Dream. She always knew when she'd had it, for she awoke in an odd state of paralysis, barely able to breath, let alone move.

Grace felt disturbed. Was she remembering something after all this time? Her therapist had said it was bound to happen one day and the sooner the better, so she could "deal with it." Grace hadn't agreed. She wasn't about to spend years in therapy feeling sorry for herself and using the past as an excuse for avoiding the future. Instead she had worked her ass off to carve out a decent career and to earn her black belt in karate.

Unsettled, Grace showered and brushed her teeth. Being a victim was a state of mind, nothing more, she reminded herself. She was physically strong and had money, assets and a job with status. No one could take those things away from her.

An hour later she was chopping papaw and bananas into a bowl. After adding thick coconut cream, she carried her breakfast out onto the verandah. Her cottage looked out across Hibiscus Bay, a picture-book setting skirted by lush, tropical greenery, waving palms, and brightly-hued cannas and hibiscus.

For a moment Grace was sorry she couldn't simply relax and enjoy it. But this was not a holiday. She had less than three weeks to complete an initial feasibility study on the conversion of the island to a toxic waste disposal site. So far it looked promising. Moon Island was the most isolated of the Cook group. It was ideal—far enough away from civilization to attract a minimum of attention and large enough to support the kind of facilities required. There was little chance of tourists stumbling on the place by accident, and hopefully Greenpeace would have better things to do raising money and saving seals than to hound a company engaged in legitimate business activity.

Argus was prepared to pay handsomely for a foothold in the region and according to Robert Hausmann, the Cook Islands' Premier was falling over backwards to accommodate them. That was hardly surprising, Grace thought with a measure of cynicism. She could imagine Argus landing the company jet at Avarua, Hausmann touring the place, endowing a hospital, building a school. Gestures of goodwill—the kind that came with a price tag.

With Hausmann handling the purchase of Moon Island, it was Grace's job to come up with recommendations for establishing deep-water access and appropriate dumping protocols. They couldn't risk destroying the reef entirely. It provided the perfect solution to the problem of pollution. A reef could easily be landfilled with nontoxic waste, and toxic materials confined to the island itself. And unlike the Marshalls, the Cook Islands weren't likely to be affected by contaminants carried downwind of the dumping zone. That was exactly the kind of embarrassing problem a reputable company like Argus took pains to avoid.

So far she had assessed the impact on the island of blasting away a portion of its coral reef to establish a passable channel, and she was now calculating the landfill capacity. Glancing through her report data, Grace made a few notes and dropped the papers on the small table beside her. Somehow she couldn't work up much enthusiasm for her job today. Perhaps it was the sunshine, the distant sound of the sea.

She scanned her surroundings. Through the dense green foliage to her right, she could just make out the thatched roof of Frangipani Cottage. She thought about its inhabitant. Dawn, the prickly young Australian, was an unexpected but pleasant distraction. Grace smiled, recalling her nakedness, the arms across the breasts, the picture of outraged virtue. Very fetching, but not very convincing. For all the protestations, those baby blue eyes were a dead giveaway. Grace never missed a sexual cue.

Getting to her feet, she smoothed her shorts. The Australian was definitely her cup of tea—young, cute and reassuringly shallow. The perfect fuck, no less. It was a pity about her legs. The scars looked recent, and she was obviously painfully self-conscious of them. It must be tough, Grace reflected. Dawn had probably been a real knockout before it happened. She still was, scars aside. But maybe she didn't see it that way.

For a moment Grace contemplated leaving the kid alone. She was a bit young and it seemed almost too easy. On the other hand, there was something very appealing about that mixture of arrogance and vulnerability. If Dawn was feeling as undesirable as Grace suspected, she would be doing her a favor. There was nothing like good sex to boost a woman's confidence.

Grace wondered idly how long it would take to get her neighbor into the sack. Three days? Less? Draining her coffee, she placed a bet with herself. That coveted new Vuitton trunk, if she could seduce Dawn Beaumont within forty-eight hours.


DAWN WAS DEEPLY enmeshed in the latest Jackie Collins novel when she heard footsteps on her verandah. There was a knock on her door, and a voice called her name.

Recognizing her neighbor's distinctive accent, she froze in her chair. What was that woman doing here? She would pretend she wasn't home, Dawn decided. Hopefully Grace Ramsay hadn't seen her through the big windows that opened onto the verandah. Dawn craned slightly to check. There was a loud thud. Dismayed, she stared down at the floor where her Jackie Collins was splayed open.

"Oh, there you are." A coppery head poked in the window.

Guilty heat flooded Dawn's cheeks. "Oh, um...hi."

"Did I wake you?" Grace asked, swinging one long leg over the windowsill and casually perching astride it. She was wearing baggy khaki shorts and a thin faded shirt. Beneath the brim of her slouch hat, her eyes shone with bold awareness.

Feeling self-conscious, Dawn said, "I was only reading."

Grace Ramsay was here out of politeness, she decided. The woman had, after all, found her passed out on the beach just the day before.

Bearing out her assumption, Grace inquired, "Are you feeling better today?"

"Yes, thank you," Dawn responded. "I think it was just sunstroke. I'm fine now."

"Great." A broad smile. Dawn didn't like the way those charcoal eyes glittered, as if Grace knew something that Dawn didn't. "How about coming on a walk? I've even packed a picnic."

A picnic! Dawn's chest constricted. Distractedly, she cast about for an excuse. "No..." She shook her head. "I don't think so. I... er..."

Grace swung her other leg over the sill and faced Dawn squarely. "It's a beautiful day out there." She adopted a persuasive tone. "Far too nice to shut yourself away with only Jackie Collins for company."

Dawn glanced ambivalently toward the paperback. Grace was right. She should be outside getting fresh air and exercise, not cooped up in her cottage doing a Greta Garbo. A picnic. It sounded harmless enough, and it wasn't as if she had other plans.

Stealing a covert look at Grace, she felt vaguely ashamed of herself. There was no need for her to be so standoffish. In fact, it was downright neurotic. The woman was only trying to be friendly. So what if she was a lesbian like Cody and Annabel? Did that make her some kind of villain?

*Grow up*, Dawn told herself. The world was full of people who were different from her. Was she planning to spend her entire life trying to avoid them? "A walk would be nice," she conceded awkwardly. "Although I can't go terribly far. I mean...my legs...I still can't—"

"I thought we'd go inland a bit." Grace acted as if there was no problem. "There's a lookout point about half an hour away. It's quite stunning up there."

"I think I know where you mean." Dawn brightened, remembering the ridge that defined the outer perimeter of the *makatea*, a fossilized coral reef that rimmed the island's interior. It was a beautiful spot. She and Cody had paused up there the day before to admire the views.

"You know the island?" Grace seemed pleased.

"I've stayed here once before."

"Then you'll be able to lead the way back if I get us lost." Grace gave a quirky little smile.

Dawn got to her feet, still vaguely dubious. Her face must have betrayed something, because Grace was suddenly serious. "If you're worried about making the distance, don't be. I can always carry you if you get tired."

She was completely serious. Tensing, Dawn recalled being carried naked in Grace's arms the day before. "I'm sure that won't be necessary," she said hastily.

Again that smile, full of wicked promise. "You never know your luck."

# Chapter
# Seven

INLAND, THE ISLAND was thickly covered in jungle. It smelled close and damp, replete with the heady scents of gardenia and frangipani. Grace halted at regular intervals to take what seemed a wasteful quantity of photos. All the same, Dawn was glad of these frequent opportunities to rest her protesting legs. This was the first time she had attempted an uphill walk of any duration, and she was managing a good deal better than she had expected.

"When were you here last?" Grace asked as they were climbing the ridge.

"Nearly three years ago." Dawn gripped Grace's arm as they picked their way slowly across the uneven terrain. It frustrated her to feel so dependent, but she was acutely conscious of the razor-sharp coral beneath the lush foliage. Her walking stick was all but useless on a hike like this.

"Have you been up on this ridge before?"

"On part of it. I've crossed the *makatea* over by Passion Bay. There are some caves in the middle of the island."

"Really?" Grace helped her over a fallen tree. "How do you get to them?"

"You'd have to ask Cody. I only went there once." Dawn stumbled, her walking stick sliding off a rock. Grace's hold on her tightened. Tensing, she found her footing and pulled quickly away. "There was a hurricane and we had to evacuate our houses and stay in one of the caves. We slept there."

"You slept with Cody? How delicious."

The comment startled Dawn, its brazen inference clear. Grace found Cody attractive and was not backward about saying so. For some reason this rankled. Dawn had a crazy urge to remind Grace that Cody already had a girlfriend—if that's what women like her called one another. Instead she kept doggedly to the conversational track. "There were four of us, actually. It was really scary. I don't like caves."

"What *do* you like, Dawn?" Grace looked back over her shoulder, her expression roguish.

Avoiding her disquieting gaze, Dawn said, "I like music." It sounded inane. She should at least have said what kind of music.

"Music," Grace echoed, shortening her stride to stay within arms reach of Dawn. "Me, too. Have you ever been to Michigan?"

It seemed a bizarre question.

"To the Womyn's Music Festival," Grace elaborated.

"No. I've only been to America for swim meets."

"You were a competitive swimmer?"

"Yes." Dawn didn't trust herself to say any more.

"Bummer." Another direct stare. "I'm sorry."

They were almost at the top of the rise, Dawn noted with relief. And a good thing, too. Her legs had coped okay until the gentle incline grew sharply steeper. Now she was on the verge of collapse. Knees wobbling, she stopped and made like she was admiring the scenery.

Grace immediately halted and extended a hand. "Come on. I'm not contagious."

Dawn tried not to read anything into that remark. "I need to challenge myself," she said, fending off assistance. "I haven't had enough exercise since the accident."

Grace searched Dawn's face. "You give yourself a hard time over this accident, don't you?"

For a moment Dawn's eyes brimmed with hot tears. Fighting them back, she said, "I'd rather not talk about it, if you don't mind."

Grace shrugged. "Suit yourself. It was just an observation." Smoothly changing the subject, she pointed toward a small clearing. "There's the lookout." Ignoring Dawn's half-hearted protests, she slipped an arm around her and assisted her along the ridge to a grassy glade.

"This is amazing," she said, easing Dawn to the ground. Strolling a few paces away, she stood on a rocky formation that overlooked the ocean on all sides. She took off her hat and slowly fanned herself. "I've never seen anything like it." There was a huskiness in her voice that hinted at tears.

Dawn was surprised to think of a worldly person like Grace getting emotional over a view of the ocean. But there was something magical about being on an island cut off from the rest of the world, not a glimpse of land in any direction. Time was meaningless. You were marooned. Gazing out at eternity.

"It's so ancient," Dawn ventured. "It's hard to imagine that anywhere else even exists."

Grace gave Dawn a strange look. "Exactly. Surreal, isn't it? Completely primeval. You can sense others have stood here, seeing what we're seeing. Feeling...insignificant."

Dawn took in the view once more. Like a braid of diamonds, the horizon shimmered, dividing ocean and sky. It was as if the island occupied some hidden dimension in a limitless blue void. "I suppose the whole world was once like this. Kind of empty..." She trailed off, conscious she sounded flaky.

"Gondwanaland." Grace flicked her a lopsided grin. "Paradise...for dinosaurs at any rate."

"Paradise." Dawn smiled. "Well, the island is supposed to be sacred."

"Ah...yes." Grace's expression altered. In a slightly mocking tone, she said, "The famous curse of Moon Island."

"You don't believe in it?"

"Let's just say, I'm not the gullible type." Removing her backpack, Grace dropped it onto the grass and sat down next to it, stretching her legs out in front of her and replacing her hat. Beneath the shady brim, her eyes sparkled. "Are you telling me you think any guy setting foot on this place is going to be struck by lightening?"

"There's a lot of stuff science can't explain," Dawn said. "In my country the Aboriginal people place curses by pointing a bone at someone. People actually die."

"There's a scientific explanation for that," Grace said. "In many cultures a person who believes he's been cursed becomes ill because he convinces himself he is doomed. It's a simple case of mind over matter...another version of the placebo effect."

"You think every mystery has an explanation?" Dawn thought it must be nice to believe in a world governed entirely by logic and common sense.

"Human beings have always created mystical explanations for what is outside their knowledge. Superstition is the fast food of the scientifically illiterate. And, of course, religious fundamentalism depends on ignorance."

"You don't believe in God?" Dawn could almost hear her parents lamenting the moral decay of civilization.

"My spiritual beliefs are irrelevant. I suppose what I'm saying is that people need explanations, but it's hard work to become fully informed. The more you learn, the more you discover things aren't always black and white. With religion or superstition, there's no need to think for yourself. Some guy in fancy headgear has done it all for you. Talk about instant gratification."

"I see what you're getting at," Dawn said, surprised to find herself having this profound discussion. "But don't you think God has a plan for us all and things happen for a reason? Like maybe God is showing us a different path, or even punishing us for something?"

Grace was silent for a moment. Gravely she met Dawn's eyes. "Do you really think the same God responsible for creation, in all its vast beauty and complexity, is nothing more than a petty tyrant who needs to flaunt his power by wrecking human lives?"

Put like that, it didn't make much sense. Dawn supposed she was just another human being trying to explain an eternal question—in her case, *why me?* "I guess I've been wondering why God did this," she said, gesturing at her legs. "Like, is there a message he's trying to send me and I'm just not getting it?"

"I understand. I really do." Grace paused, as if weighing her next words carefully. "Listen. Something very bad once happened to me, and for a long time I asked the same questions you're asking. I mean who wants to suffer if there's no good reason for it?"

"Not me." Dawn interjected, with a small, bitter laugh.

Grace pulled a picnic blanket from her pack. "In the end, I decided I was in the wrong place at the wrong time. Shit happens."

"It was just bad luck?"

"Yep," Grace said, spreading the blanket over the ground. "Here, get comfortable."

Dawn inched across, occupying a narrow strip of soft cotton. Grace gave her an odd look, then sat a couple of feet away. "So you're saying what happened to you was completely random?" Dawn asked.

"Essentially, yes." Grace stretched out her legs and lay down, linking her hands behind her head.

Despite her slenderness, she looked very strong, Dawn thought, eyeing her lithe, muscular thighs and the solid smoothness of her arms and shoulders. Somehow Grace didn't fit Dawn's image of a scientist: a mouse-like person wearing thick glasses and a white coat. Her thoughts returned to their conversation. Her own accident was not random.

"My accident wasn't bad luck," Dawn said. "It was my own fault."

Grace studied her for a moment. "Dawn, there's a big difference between blaming yourself, and taking responsibility for your choices. Do you understand?"

"It seems like splitting hairs."

"One is about guilt, the other is about being honest with

yourself."

Tears flooded Dawn's eyes. "I'll never forgive myself for what I did."

Grace gazed at her. Sounding terribly sad all of a sudden, she said, "Yes, that is the hard part." She seemed about to say something else, but her charcoal eyes grew shuttered.

An awkward silence followed. Grace seemed prickly, her discomfort palpable. Dawn guessed her change of mood must be something to do with the bad thing that had happened to her. Wondering what it was, but sensing Grace did not want to talk about it, Dawn groped for something appropriate to say.

In the end, Grace spared her the trouble, apparently making a conscious attempt to lighten up. "I don't know about you, but I'm ravenous," she said, lifting an assortment of plastic containers from her pack. "Hungry?"

"Not really. I'm feeling a bit sick."

"Drink this." Grace placed a bottle of Gatorade in Dawn's hands. In a no-nonsense tone, she said, "We're not going anywhere until you've eaten something. So don't even think about standing up. Okay?"

Blinking, Dawn drank the sweet liquid. Then, to her surprise, she consumed an enormous quantity of food over the next hour. Other than the meal at Cody's place the night before, she had barely eaten since she arrived.

Even Grace seemed impressed. "Much better. You're not so pale now." Stretching like a contented feline, Grace lay back on the blanket, unbuttoning her shirt and pulling it from her khaki shorts. With a languid sigh, she closed her eyes and spread her shirt open, exposing her skin to the sun.

Her breasts and torso were like the rest of her, smooth and tanned. Obviously she sunbathed half naked all the time. Dawn's eyes were drawn to Grace's nipples. They were small and the color of dark toffee. For far too long Dawn stared at them, her breathing strangely affected.

She felt clammy. Was she going to be sick? Had the climb been too much? Forcing her attention back to the scenery, she mentally framed a polite request to return home. It's not like she would be inventing excuses. She really was feeling ill. Her gaze returned to her companion. Her heart skipped a beat.

Grace was staring straight up at her. "You okay?" she enquired in a silky tone. Their eyes locked for what seemed an eternity.

Dawn averted her head. "Just thirsty." She unscrewed her water flask and made a show of drinking.

"How old are you, Dawn?" Grace asked.

"Twenty-two."

"God, that's young."

Dawn lifted her chin. "How old are you?"

"Thirty-two. And I live in New York, so you can add a hundred years to that."

"It's that bad?"

"It depends who you are and how much money you have." Grace sat up, linking her arms around her knees. "So, tell me," She shot Dawn a challenging look. "Are you involved with anyone at the moment?"

The question took Dawn by surprise. Despite the warmth of the afternoon sun, her skin goose-bumped. "Not right now."

"Neither am I."

Dawn hoped that was all Grace planned to say. She had no intention of getting into all that personal stuff with a stranger. With a glance at her wristwatch, she said, "We should be getting back soon."

"What's the hurry? Got a big date tonight?"

"As if," Dawn muttered.

Grace grinned, her eyes teasing. "I guess you have to beat them off with a club in Sydney."

Dawn couldn't tell if Grace was serious or making fun of her. "I've never had time for that kind of thing," she said. Her throat felt tight. It was all she could do not to fixate on the band of bronzed flesh exposed where Grace's shirt parted.

"You do now," Grace noted with a languid smile.

Dawn cast a sharp look at the scars down each leg. Her mouth shook.

"Shit, Dawn." Grace followed the direction of her gaze. "I didn't mean it like that." She placed a hand on Dawn's arm. "I was talking about being here on the island. You know...so much time, so little to do."

"I get it." Dawn's skin burned from the fleeting pressure of Grace's fingers. She'd had enough deep and meaningful conversation for one day, she decided. With faltering hands, she started packing up their picnic things.

"I'll do that." Grace buttoned her shirt. Cautiously, she said, "Dawn, I'm sorry. I know it's a touchy subject."

"Forget it, Grace. It's no big deal." Screening her muddled feelings with a breezy smile, she added, "It's time I got out of the sun, that's all. After yesterday—"

"Sure. Makes sense." Grace stuffed everything into her pack and tied it down. "We could go back to my place for a while. Want to do that?"

Dawn lifted her eyes, only to find them drawn relentlessly

to the outline of Grace's nipples against her thin cotton shirt. In the grip of a peculiar fascination, she proceeded up Grace's body, pausing at the hollow of her throat, the wide sensual mouth.

"Is that a yes?" Grace asked.

Something in her tone made Dawn's nerves leap. Frowning, she stared down at the scars on her hands. What was wrong with her? Why was she staring at this woman's body like it was the first she had ever seen? Unsettled, she said, "I'm kind of tired. Maybe another time."

"No problem." Grace was suddenly businesslike, gathering their belongings and passing Dawn her stick. With a quick glance at Dawn's legs, she said, "I probably shouldn't have dragged you up here. But you seemed kind of down. I thought you might enjoy it."

"I did," Dawn hastened to say. "I have... It's just..." How could she explain her uneasiness about going back to Grace's place? It was completely illogical, like most of her feelings these days.

"I think I know what you're saying." Grace's expression was disarmingly frank. "Don't look so worried. Everything's fine." She stroked Dawn's cheek and gently cupped her chin. Leaning closer, she brushed Dawn's mouth with her own, so lightly Dawn barely had time to register the touch.

Throughout the slow hike back to Frangipani Cottage, Dawn's face burned and an oily nausea made her stomach crawl. Grace Ramsay had kissed her. *On the mouth.* No matter how hard she tried, she could not convince herself that this was merely an American way of being friendly. Neither could she make sense of her own reactions to this woman.

Scared suddenly, she wished she could run far, far away— from the island, from Grace Ramsay, and from her own deafening heartbeat.

# Chapter
# Eight


"DAWN! IT'S ME, Cody." Footsteps halted on the verandah outside her bedroom window.

Dawn dragged herself out of bed, pulled on a sarong, and padded out, blinking in the buttercup light of morning.

Cody was standing on her verandah in a bedraggled straw hat and well worn cut-off jeans. "Fancy a spot of fishing?" she said.

"Fishing?" Dawn wrinkled her nose and considered the prospect of chopping up bait, gaffing fish and watching their tails thrash as life departed.

She shook her head. "Not really my thing. I mean, ick."

Cody eyed her knowingly. "I'll do the nasty stuff. You can just sit there and hold on to a rod."

"Won't I be in the way?"

"Of course not. You'll balance the boat."

"Thanks a million. Now I feel really wanted."

Cody grinned at her. "Bring plenty of sun block. It gets hot out there."

She wasn't kidding. Cody's boat was a sixteen-foot runabout with a Mercury outboard. Its shallow canopy offered some protection from the merciless sun, but after a couple of hours, Dawn's T-shirt was wet with sweat and her arms and legs were slick beneath the sun block she'd plastered on. They hadn't had a single bite.

Dawn adjusted her hat so the brim shadowed her neck more effectively. "They know it's me," she said crossly. "They know I hate catching them."

"You're talking about our dinner," Cody said. "I can't go home empty-handed. Annabel will kill me."

She said it so easily, so naturally, Dawn found herself staring. "Cody," she began in a thin little voice. "How did you know you were...you know...gay?"

Cody lowered her rod. Her expression shifted from startled

incomprehension to composure, as if she had willed herself not to react. "Why do you ask?"

Dawn was glad she could hide her own embarrassment behind her sunglasses. "I just wondered. I'm sorry. You don't have to answer. It's none of my business."

Cody shrugged. "I don't mind." Adjusting her rod, she looked out at the hazy ocean. "It was a very long time ago, and it wasn't exactly a lightning bolt. I guess I knew I was a lesbian before I ever heard the word."

"What do you mean?"

"I've always had feelings for women, even as a kid. I always had a crush on someone."

"But that's normal, isn't it?" Dawn said, "I mean phases—they're a part of development."

"Well, there are two schools of thought on that. A lot of people believe we have no way of knowing what is normal until we stop pressuring young people so hard to be heterosexual."

"I don't feel pressured," Dawn objected.

"I see," Cody said blandly. "So you think it's perfectly okay for people to be gay? If you woke up tomorrow morning and saw lesbian printed on your forehead, you'd feel fine about walking downtown."

"Of course not," Dawn retorted.

"But you don't think that constitutes pressure?"

Looking at it that way, it was pressure, Dawn supposed. But then, being homosexual wasn't normal. In some places it wasn't even legal.

"Have you ever noticed that some people really hate gays?" Cody persisted. "Don't you think some of us might feel like we have a disease and maybe we should start going out with the opposite sex so people won't notice?"

Dawn changed hands on her rod, wiping one wet palm on her shorts. "Is that what you did?" she asked huskily.

"For a while," Cody admitted. "But I was lucky. I ended up dating boys who were a bit like me. Safe company..."

"Then you just started dating girls?"

"I guess you could say that. I fell in love a few times before I got into a relationship."

"Have you had a lot of...um...relationships?" Dawn felt herself blush.

"Dawn!" Cody said with a laugh. "I think we've taken show and tell far enough for one day."

"I'm sorry, I didn't mean it like that. I meant—Cody," she blurted. "Do you hate men?"

Cody laughed, a deep warm laugh. "Hate men? I'm not

really interested enough in men to hate them."

Her comment startled Dawn—it echoed her own feelings so closely. Flustered, she adjusted the tension on her line and wiggled the hook experimentally. "But have you ever...um."

"Have I ever had a sexual relationship with a man? No, in a word."

"Then how do you know you're a lesbian?"

"How do you know you're straight?" Cody fired back. "Have you ever slept with a woman?"

Dawn blushed even more. She didn't want to think about yesterday, about Grace Ramsay sprawled on that picnic blanket, flaunting her body. Besides, nothing had happened but a simple, friendly little kiss. That was all. She squirmed in her seat. "It doesn't matter which way you look at it, Cody. We've got two sexes, right? Male and female. And nature attracts them to each other so that the human race continues. If everyone was homosexual, there'd be no more babies."

"I think you're mixing procreation with recreation. Do you only want sex when you're planning on having a baby?"

Dawn looked away. "Sex isn't that great," she muttered. "I can take it or leave it."

"I can't," Cody said flatly, and Dawn's mouth parted with shock.

Suddenly she found herself imagining it was Cody yesterday, not Grace. She imagined more than a mere brush of the lips. Instead, a kiss like the one she had seen Cody and Annabel exchange that day on the beach years ago. The thought made her nipples harden. Horrified, she hunched her shoulders and stared morosely at her feet. How could she entertain that thought even for a second?

"Sex is wonderful," Cody said. "Especially when you're in love."

Dawn couldn't look up. She felt cornered, confused. She wasn't in love with Nigel. She had never been in love with anyone. What was love, anyway? A racing heart, the sun setting on a tropical beach, violins playing. Was it sex on car seats, an engagement ring people stared at?

She couldn't begin to imagine having the kind of feelings Cody was talking about. Maybe that was why sex had never interested her that much. She thought about Grace Ramsay again and suddenly wondered what would have happened had she returned that fleeting kiss.

Swinging her gaze back to Cody, she asked clumsily, "What do lesbians do—" Her line gave a sharp wrench, and she clutched her rod, shouting, "I've got one. I've got one."

She staggered to her feet only to be pushed straight back down onto the padded bench. Cody was beside her, locking the rod into the grips and adjusting the reel.

"Let it run," she said as the line screamed from the rod, yard after yard. "It's a biggie."

She secured a safety belt around Dawn's waist then scampered down to the stern, starting the outboard and hurling instructions at Dawn. The minutes ticked by, Dawn winding and winding, the boat dragging its anchor. The fish stayed on. Gradually, inch by inch it drew closer, then hurtled off toward the open sea again.

"I don't believe this," Cody said after it had made what felt like its thousandth bid for freedom.

"My arms are going to fall off," Dawn wailed. "It feels like we've got bloody Jaws on there."

Cody grinned, but there was a seriousness in the set of her mouth. "Maybe we have. I'll take over, if you like."

"No! I'm perfectly capable of catching a goddamn fish by myself." Dawn started winding anew, sweating and grunting, swearing under her breath.

Cody looked at her watch. "It's been on more than an hour."

Dawn traced the line out. The water sparkled bright turquoise. She was certain she caught a glimpse of something beneath the surface. "Look!" she yelled. About twenty feet from the boat the sea exploded and a huge silver fish twisted into the air.

"Shit! " Cody gasped. "A marlin."

Dawn panted with the strain of its weight on the line. "It's enormous."

"Roll on dinner." Cody rubbed her hands. "Keep on winding."

"I am bloody winding." Dawn felt as if she'd been hauling on that reel forever. The line was unbearably heavy. Her muscles screamed in violent protest.

Cody clipped herself to the safety line at the stern of the boat and perched there with a long spike in her hand. A silvery head rose from the water, swinging back and forth, a straining body gleamed in the sun.

Dawn looked down into a black sorrowful eye. "No!" she screamed as Cody lifted the gaffe high. "Please! Don't kill it."

Cody stared at her, uncomprehending, then lowered the gaffe, groped in the bag at her feet and produced a set of pliers. Suspended over the edge of the boat, fending off the fish's sword, she strained down and snapped the hook cleanly apart.

Seconds later a tail broke the surface of the water and the

marlin vanished.

They both stared after it, Dawn releasing sharp exhausted pants, Cody quiet and stunned.

"No one's ever going to believe us," Cody finally said.

Dawn shrugged. "The fish knows."

# Chapter Nine

THE NEXT MORNING, Dawn awoke to the sound of her name being called. Blinking, she propped herself on her elbows and cocked her head.

"Dawn!" Someone was knocking on her door.

Opening the window beside her bed, she peered out.

Grace Ramsay was standing on the verandah. "Oh, hell." Grace looked embarrassed. "Did I wake you?"

"I think I overslept," Yawning, Dawn glanced at the clock on her dressing table. Midday! She had slept for nearly eighteen hours. It was the best sleep she'd had in months—since the accident, in fact.

"I'll come back later."

"No," Dawn said quickly. "It's okay. I'll get up now." Lowering her feet to the floor, she gathered up a sarong, wrapped it around herself and reached automatically for her pills. She twisted the cap then hesitated. Her legs felt surprisingly strong, the usual aching less pronounced. Hardly daring to believe her good fortune, she replaced the pill bottle and went to open the French doors.

Grace was reclining on the sunny wooden steps, her T-shirt damply outlining her breasts and shoulders. "I saw you out on the bay yesterday," she said as Dawn emerged. "Shame you lost that fish. You did really well holding on so long." Her eyes were concealed behind dark lenses. "I was impressed."

Her throat looked very soft. A tiny dark mole nestled in the shadow of her left collarbone. Dawn experienced an odd desire to touch it. Feeling self-conscious, she blurted, "I don't much like fishing. It seems cruel."

"Then you're not sorry you lost the fish after all?" Grace's voice was faintly teasing.

"It never did me any harm. Why kill it?"

Grace removed her sunglasses. "Now don't tell me you collect for Greenpeace, Dawn." Her voice held a trace of cynicism.

"What's wrong with Greenpeace? At least they're doing something to stop us wrecking this planet." Dawn stopped, conscious of a sudden edge of discomfort about her visitor. What was Grace doing here so early? Had she simply come over to pass the time of day talking about fishing? Straightening, she said, "I need to take a shower. Is there something you wanted?"

"I was wondering if you have plans for this afternoon?"

Dawn's heart sank. Clearly Grace was about to offer some kind of invitation. Remembering the awkward picnic, she said, "I've got some letters to write, and I thought I'd do some reading."

Grace sought out her eyes. "So, is anyone cooking you dinner?"

Dawn felt color drift into her cheeks. Avoiding Grace's gaze, she tried to decipher the motivation behind these overtures of friendship. Perhaps Grace was simply a social kind of person, or maybe she was bored, stuck out here on an island when she was obviously used to a huge city. Or maybe she just felt sorry for Dawn.

Grace appeared to draw her own conclusions from Dawn's silence. With a casual shrug, she said, "Okay, so you don't feel like company right now. I'll be home later if you change your mind. Just come on over." She started down the steps, then paused, adding softly, "I'd really like to see you, Dawn."

The dinner invitation plagued Dawn throughout the afternoon. Lying on the beach, her discarded Jackie Collins sticky with tanning lotion, she wondered why on earth Grace would want to spend time with her. It wasn't as if they had anything in common apart from occupying neighboring cottages. And she was certain Grace had no idea of her athletic fame back in Australia. Even if she did, Dawn could not imagine that factoring into her friendly overtures.

Her mind drifted to the picnic, to the way Grace had stared at her, and that one tiny kiss. Perhaps she was being paranoid about it, attributing ridiculous significance to a meaningless social gesture. On the other hand, Dawn strongly suspected Grace was a lesbian. And what if she was? Did that change anything?

Yes, it did, she conceded miserably. Fanning herself with her paperback, she recalled her conversation on the boat with Cody. She was prejudiced, she realized. She was one of those people who snickered at gay jokes and made gay people feel bad about themselves. She had joined in when everyone victimized a girl on the swim team they suspected of being gay.

Dawn felt sick thinking about the way they had behaved. In

the end, they had driven Carmen off the team—out of swimming altogether. The irony struck Dawn like a battering ram. Carmen had been deprived of her chance at Olympic glory, and now Dawn's career was over, too. Was the accident some kind of poetic justice? Was this God's message?

Dawn started to cry. When she got back to Sydney, she was going to go see Carmen, she decided. She would apologize and offer to go with her to swim meets as a personal trainer so she could sit in the change rooms. No one would dare hassle Carmen then. Feeling better, she wiped her face, gathered up her possessions and started back to Frangipani Cottage.

The sun was a fading bloom on the horizon, and the familiar cadence of the jungle had given way to the frenetic sounds of dusk. It would be dark soon. She would light the lamps in her cottage and sit alone, probably feeling sorry for herself and wondering what to do with her life. And when there seemed no point in sitting up any longer, she would shower, take her pills, and go to bed wondering about the point of it all.

Impulsively, Dawn opened her closet and stared at the small collection of clothes hanging there. *Why not have dinner with Grace Ramsay?* She had taken a dislike to the woman for no other reason than it seemed she might be a lesbian. How immature. How pathetic.

Ashamed of herself, Dawn pulled out one of the more appealing sundresses Trish had insisted she pack. Somehow she hadn't been able to bring herself to wear it yet. It seemed too bright with its yellow background and big red flowers. Dawn showered, put it on and studied herself critically.

The dress was close-fitting and short—too short perhaps. Dawn fingered the scarred flesh of her thighs. At least she'd tanned a little since she'd been on the island, and her muscles had regained some of their tone. Maybe she looked all right after all. Frowning, she brushed out her hair and put on a little lip gloss, leaving the rest of her face bare of makeup. It didn't matter what she looked like; she was only having dinner with a woman.

Dawn wrapped a few painkillers in a tissue, slid this into her bra, and applied a little Samsara to each wrist. Glancing in the mirror once more, she felt a flash of pleasure. She could have been looking at her old self. If it weren't for her legs, and...there was something about her face, too.

Dawn studied her image, unable to figure out what was different. It was her eyebrows, she finally concluded. She hadn't plucked them in months.

"Tough," she said aloud. Facial torture—who needed it?

"YOU LOOK GREAT." Grace greeted her with a candid smile. "I was hoping you'd come. I'd have a hell of a lot to eat if you didn't." Leading Dawn into the sitting room, she said, "Make yourself comfortable. Can I get you a drink?"

Dawn asked for fruit juice. Alcohol didn't combine well with painkillers. Her eyes were drawn to the dining table. Apparently Grace had been pretty sure she would not be eating alone. Places were set for two. There were freshly picked flowers and flickering candles. It was very simple, but it was also...romantic. Disconcerted, Dawn shot a surreptitious look in Grace's direction.

A smart, attractive woman like her could probably get anyone she wanted, lesbian or not. It was absurd to imagine she might have designs on a twenty-two year old with no job and a pill problem. Dawn was kidding herself if she imagined Grace posed any kind of threat to her heterosexual virtue. Ignoring a flurry of nervousness that knotted her stomach, she inquired lamely, "How is your work going?"

"I'm pleased so far." Grace handed her a tall glass and joined her on the sofa. "I have a report to finish in the next few days, then maybe I'll get some time to play."

"What do you like to do...for play?"

"I like to get physical." Grace paused very deliberately, then explained, "Squash, skiing, swimming. How about you?"

"I... Well, now that I don't swim, I..." Dawn's mouth started to tremble.

Grace shook her head in self-deprecation. "I'm always putting my foot in it with you."

Dawn didn't trust herself to speak, instead producing a wan smile and a dismissive shrug.

"How about this—if I promise not to mention swimming all evening, will you stay for dinner?" Grace's sweet, teasing tone was infectious.

Dawn smiled back at her. "Sure. Why not?"

"Good. Then let's eat."

Dawn took the hand Grace extended and allowed herself to be led to the table. Grace pulled a chair out for her and, with an air of cheeky ceremony, opened a bottle of champagne and filled Dawn's glass before her own.

"Did I mention you look beautiful?" she said, sitting down and raising her wine in a playful toast. "Let's drink to that."

Dawn found herself blushing as she swallowed the tingling champagne. "I'm not supposed to drink alcohol."

"For religious reasons?" Her tone was mock-serious.

"No." Dawn giggled. "I'm on drugs."

"And you didn't offer to share." Grace continued her playful banter. "I thought you liked me."

"Not that kind of drugs!" Dawn said and fished around inside her bra. "These." She opened the tissue to display her pills.

"My God," Grace said. "Elephant tranquilizers." She looked at Dawn, eyes penetrating. "Is the pain still that bad?"

"You get used to it," Dawn said. "I have this fantasy that one day I'll wake up, and everything will be back to normal. I'll get out of bed and I won't even feel my legs. It'll be so comfortable and easy walking around." She took a gulp of champagne. "I never knew how much I took for granted until this happened. It makes you think."

"About?"

"About how lucky you are. It could have been a lot worse. At least I *can* walk." Dawn fell silent, conscious of a change in her outlook, yet unsure how exactly it had come about. "To be honest, I've been wallowing in self-pity ever since it happened."

"I can relate," Grace said. Folding Dawn's pills into a neat little package, she slid them back across the table. "Grief is natural. It takes its course, then we move on."

*Move on—to what?* Dawn served herself from the platter Grace offered. The meal was delicious—fish marinated in coconut milk, steamed rice, salad. She chewed a few bites, seduced by the subtle but tangy combination of flavors. "I'm not sure what I'm going to do now," she admitted eventually. "My whole life has revolved around swimming ever since I was a little kid."

"Are you trained for anything else?"

Dawn paused between succulent mouthfuls. "I was training as a kindergarten teacher."

Apparently, Grace noticed her lackluster tone. "A kindergarten teacher? You don't strike me as the little-kids type."

Dawn grimaced. "I'm not. I sort of had to do it." She fell silent, trying to figure out a way to change the subject. She'd had a swimming scholarship, and it was a toss between the evils of accounting, high school teaching, or kindergarten. "I still have a year of school left, but I don't think I want to carry on. How about you? Did you always want to be a scientist?"

Grace smiled, her chin propped against her hand. "Well, when I was a kid I had grandiose ideas about making some earth-shattering discovery and getting a Nobel Prize. I guess I took it from there."

"Do you think you might? Make a famous discovery, I mean." Dawn was slightly awestruck. Despite their previous conversation, she felt none the wiser about what Grace actually did. The woman was probably some kind of genius.

Grace was laughing, but her expression was cynical. "Hell, no. I live in the real world now. Research science is all very glamorous, but the pay isn't. Women are seldom credited for what we achieve. Look at DNA. Did Rosalind Franklin get the Nobel Prize? No, the boys did. I'm damned if I'm going to work my ass off so some man can get his name in the journals."

"That's exactly what happens in sports, too," Dawn said. "Back home, if a bloke wins a final, he's a hero—plastered all over the newspapers, car endorsements, lunch with the Prime Minister. A woman does the same thing and she's lucky to get her competition airfare paid and a couple of lines on the back page." Dawn paused for a moment. She'd lost count of the times the girls on the swim team were left out of public relations events and newspaper coverage. "I guess it takes a long time for some things to change. I mean, women still can't even turn professional in a lot of sports."

"There's no point waiting around for men to cut us a bigger slice of the pie," Grace said cynically. "We have to make it happen for ourselves. That's why so many women set up their own businesses."

"Is that what you did?"

"Pretty much. I developed a scarce skill set and became a consultant. These days I hire some of the men I used to work for."

"That's great," Dawn said, thinking how smart Grace must be.

"You should consider running a business," Grace said in a thoughtful voice. "In your field you could become an agent. You say women get a shitty deal. Take on a bunch of them as clients. Everything is about money, Dawn, and women are huge consumers. Big advertisers know that. You could offer a whole stable of female athletes."

Dawn blinked. "I'm too young to do something like that. No one would take me seriously."

"So go to an agency that knows you and join the firm. Learn the business. Then leave and take all your clients with you. People do it every day."

Dawn felt awestruck. This was good advice. Her aborted swimming career had left plenty of doors open. Why not use her contacts? "I know a lot of people," she said, feeling a flare of optimism.

"So pick up the phone when you get home. You're a strong woman. Don't let this thing beat you."

Dawn felt strangely light. For the first time since the accident, she could imagine a future for herself. Even if she didn't do exactly what Grace suggested, she could see that her life held possibilities. All she had to do was open her mind to them. Conscious of Grace's steady gaze, she said, almost sheepishly, "You're giving me a pep talk."

A warm natural smile lit Grace's features. For a moment, she looked very young, her eyes soft, her head slightly cocked. "Is it working?"

Seized by an impulse, Dawn reached across the table and squeezed Grace's hand. "Yes."

Before she could withdraw, Grace caught her hand gently but firmly. Her fingers traced the pink scars that knotted the skin across Dawn's knuckles. The thin new skin was exquisitely sensitive, almost painful to touch. Shivering, Dawn gazed at the intersection of their flesh, her own a mottled latticework of colors against the smooth, slender perfection of Grace's fingers.

Grace kept her nails sensibly short, Dawn noticed. They were well manicured, the moons apparent. By contrast, her own nails were unkempt, the cuticles ragged, and several gnawed down to the quick. She lifted her eyes and found Grace gazing at her with an odd expression.

Almost immediately the good-humored indulgence returned to Grace's face. "I'm going to miss food like this when I go home," she remarked, diffusing the tension that prickled between them. "Mangos for breakfast, papayas all over the ground..."

"I'll miss the peace," Dawn said.

"It's quite a culture shock after the city, isn't it?"

"Where exactly do you live?" Dawn asked. She remembered Grace was from New York, but that was a big place.

"When I'm not in a hotel room in the likes of Bombay or Phnom Penh, I have an apartment in the West Village. Do you know New York City?"

Dawn shook her head. "Only from taxi rides. I've never spent any time sight-seeing. "

"Then you should book yourself a vacation some time. I could show you around a few places."

Dawn's pulse leapt. This was one of those friendly but insincere offers people made in the certainty they would never have to make good. She smiled all the same, charmed for a moment by the idea of exploring a thrilling new place with Grace her guide.

"I'm serious," Grace said, as if sensing Dawn doubted her. Retreating to the kitchen to brew some coffee, she added with a wicked glint, "I'd only corrupt you if you asked nicely."

Dawn laughed. "You must think I'm so...that I don't know anything."

Grace raised her eyebrows. "Are you trying to tell me you're a woman of the world, Dawn?"

Dawn felt color invade her cheeks. She lowered her eyes, immediately self-conscious. What was she trying to say, exactly? It almost sounded like she was flirting with Grace. Troubled, she checked her watch and said, "I should be going soon."

"Another tough day ahead?" Grace teased. "Sunbathing, reading... It's a dirty job, huh?"

Dawn smiled wryly. "I'm coping. Just." It was not easy to change the training habits of a lifetime. She still found it almost impossible to sleep past five a.m., that's if she managed to sleep at all. Since the accident, it had not been easy, although that seemed to be changing here on the island. "It feels pretty weird loafing on a beach instead of swimming laps," she said.

"Notice I'm not commenting on the forbidden topic," Grace bantered gently.

Dawn could not help but respond in kind. "You've been very, very good."

"I manage when the bar is set low enough." Her tone was laced with irony.

"I've had a very nice evening," Dawn said. "But it's getting late, and I know you've got work to do tomorrow."

Grace studied her with perceptive eyes. "Now there you go, looking sad again. I wish I could flatter myself that you're truly sorry to be leaving my charming company. But we both know that's not the case." She grinned suddenly, coaxingly. "Just a thought...if you stayed, we could plan your future some more over breakfast."

Dawn stiffened. *Stayed?* What did Grace mean by that? Some kind of friendly sleep-over? Or was it quite a different kind of invitation? Dawn's heart jumped in her chest, and she gazed uncertainly at the woman beside her, noticing the watchful intensity of her regard, the faint curve of her mouth. "No," she said hastily. "Um...thank you. I can find my own way back. You don't have to walk me."

"That's a matter of opinion." All nonchalance, Grace stood and offered her hand. "Shall we?"


THE VELVET NIGHT air was warm and redolent with a mix of fragrances, the heady florals now so familiar to Dawn, and a spicier scent she recognized as Grace's. Bled of color, the jungle looked dark and impenetrable. A bright full moon illuminated the monochrome world below.

Negotiating the narrow path to Frangipani Cottage, Dawn

felt oddly chagrined that Grace seemed quite content to take her home. Part of her wished she had abandoned her paranoid mis-givings and agreed to spend the night. What was the worst thing that could have happened? An unsettling image sprang to mind—herself in Grace's arms, the two of them kissing.

Dawn felt queasily conscious of Grace's hand, holding hers, of her nearness. Just an extra step or a stumble, and their bodies would collide. She rejected the thought with ruthless self-con-demnation. What was wrong with her? Why was she curious about gayness all of a sudden?

She cast her mind back to the fishing expedition with Cody. She had wanted to ask even more questions about what it was like to be a lesbian. Cody seemed to think her interest in the topic was perfectly normal. Mature adults could discuss sexual-ity without making a big deal of it. This was not High School.

As they emerged from a dense canopy of palms and vines, into a clearing a few minutes away from the cottage, Grace halted. "Do you smell that?" she asked.

Inhaling deeply, Dawn was astonished. A hypnotic scent drenched the humid night air. "What is it?"

"I think it's Night Queen. Bludgeons the senses, doesn't it?" Grace released Dawn's hand and took a few steps to the edge of the jungle. Between audibly drawn breaths, she said, "It's a rare lily species that takes a hundred years to flower. And you can only smell it at night. During the day it doesn't release its scent."

"Wow." Dawn had never heard of such a thing. "It's incredi-ble. Kind of like violets and fresh cookies and something else."

"Boronia," Grace supplied, pacing slowly around the perim-eters of the clearing. "Violets, boronia, sweet almond, and musk. I wish I could find the plant. I've smelled it each time I walk this path. But when I come back here in daylight, the scent has gone. Without it, there's no way to track down the plant."

Dawn was impressed. A plant that released its fragrance only under cover of darkness. What a remarkable theft deterrent. Nature was smart that way. "Imagine having one in your gar-den," she marveled. "You could die before you ever saw it flower."

Grace's smile was just visible in the moonlight. "The perfect gift for the masochist who has everything," she said and van-ished into a thicket of banana palms. "It seems stronger over here. Come and smell this."

Dawn insinuated herself through a gap between fleshy fronds and took another deep breath, drowning her senses in the once-in-a-lifetime scent. "I think you're right," she said. "But we'll never find it. I can't see a bloody thing."

Grace's hand took hers. Guiding Dawn back to the moonlit clearing, she said, "I'll come back in the morning and take a closer look."

"What will you do if you find it?"

"Take a sample. There are bound to be some non-flowering specimens around it." Grace pushed a stray curl off Dawn's forehead, her fingers drifting out of contact then returning to linger for a moment on Dawn's hair. In the moonlight, her face was all shadows, eyes gleaming like onyx.

Transfixed, Dawn stared at her, and it seemed they were enveloped by a profound silence, a lull in the deliberations of nature. As if from a great distance, a voice within told Dawn to turn and walk, but she felt rooted to the spot, unwilling to move, to speak, to disturb in any way the fragile synthesis of that moment. Bodies barely touching, they swayed slightly toward one another. Their mouths brushed lightly once, and again, more deliberately, joining in sweet contract.

Dawn began to tremble. She was conscious of her lips parting, her eyes closing, her body seeking Grace's. The flat of Grace's hand burned where it rested against Dawn's back. Their breasts, bellies, and thighs seemed glued. Grace's mouth, sealed hotly to Dawn's, sent shockwaves of awareness through Dawn's limbs. Bones quivering, she returned the intoxicating kiss, timidly at first, then chaotically.

Dawn was aware of her dress being unzipped, of Grace's flesh sculpting to hers, of a confusion of scents—febrile jungle, cloves, the decadent Night Queen lily. She felt weak and heavy, as if it were honey, not blood, that oozed through her veins. Responding to the coaxing pressure of Grace's tongue, she invited her deeper, until it seemed they were pouring into one another. It was a kiss like none she had ever experienced, speaking to an inner-self Dawn never knew existed.

Grace's hands slid beneath Dawn's sundress, gently, pervasively exploring her body, stealing away her brief, instinctive resistance. The sensations were unbearable, setting off a trail of tiny explosions beneath Dawn's skin. Her breasts felt heavy, the skin drawn tight. Her nipples were so exquisitely tender, she almost cried out when Grace took one between her fingers. Pulling, teasing, Grace worked one knotted nipple, then the other, taking Dawn's breasts in her hands, squeezing and kneading.

Still kissing, they sank onto the damp grass, rolling hard against one another, thighs locked. Abandoning Dawn's breasts for a moment, Grace twisted her fingers into Dawn's hair and held her still. Their kiss grew softer, until their lips barely fluttered against one another. Faces close, breath merging, they exchanged tiny, succulent kisses, roaming from cheek to throat to shoulder, tasting and kissing and biting.

Grace drew Dawn's sundress off her shoulders, caressing her throat with delicate fingers. Easing the unwanted garment down Dawn's body, she claimed the freshly exposed flesh with her mouth. Taking a nipple between her teeth, she softly tugged and sucked until Dawn could bear no more. Releasing a pent-up moan of pleasure, Dawn slid urging fingers into Grace's hair.

"Apparently you like this." Grace remarked huskily, forsaking Dawn's breasts to caress her belly and hips, and finally removing the bunched sundress altogether.

Blood pounded in Dawn's ears as she felt her panties sliding down, her thighs parted, the damp flesh between them exposed to the night air and Grace's caresses.

"Mmm...you're so wet." Grace sighed.

Dawn's eyes flew open. Grace was touching her where it was all slippery and melting, her fingers sliding back and forth. A paralyzing realization swept Dawn. She was allowing this to happen! "No!" She reached down, tearing Grace's hand away. "Stop! Please."

"Baby, what is it?" Grace withdrew instantly and changed position, propping herself on an elbow.

Dawn struggled into sitting position, grabbing her dress, heat flooding her face. Clamping her thighs together, she jerked her head to one side, deeply ashamed. What in God's name was she thinking, letting a woman touch her like that, encouraging her? She must be insane.

"Was it something I did?" Grace sounded perplexed. "Am I going too fast for you?" She reached for Dawn, freezing when she was pushed away.

"Don't touch me!" Dawn cried.

"I don't get it. What's happening here?"

"Can't you take no for an answer?"

"I wasn't hearing no from you, Dawn," Grace said. "You wanted this just as much as I did."

Tears of humiliation stung Dawn's eyes. "I did not!"

"How can you say that?" Grace shook her head, frustration entering her tone. "You're incredibly aroused. Please, tell me what this is about. Is it because of your legs?"

"No! It's nothing to do with my legs!" Dawn scrambled to her feet, dragging her dress on and wrenching the straps into place. "For God's sake, just leave me alone. There's nothing wrong with me! At least I'm normal."

Grace's gaze was black and piercing. "Let me get something clear," she said in a strained voice. "Are you a lesbian, Dawn?"

"Of course not!" Dawn hurled at her.

"Well, fuck me. I don't believe this." Laughing mirthlessly, Grace set about buttoning her shirt. "Kid," she addressed Dawn with deep irony, "if you're straight, I'm from Mars."

"Shut up!" Dawn shouted, backing away. "How could you do those disgusting things to me, then act like I'm the one with the problem!"

"You enjoyed those disgusting things," Grace yelled after her. "And if you weren't so damned hung-up, you could have enjoyed a whole lot more of them. You wanted me to fuck you. You were just about begging for it."

"That's a filthy lie." Dawn covered her ears. "I hated it, and I hate you, too."

"Fine," Grace said. "After that little episode the feeling's quite mutual. C'mon. I'll walk you home." Shoulders very stiff, she strode off into the jungle, calling carelessly, "Are you coming?" She paused, laughing harshly. "No, of course you're not. It would be too much like having a good time, wouldn't it?"

"Shut up, you...you bitch!" Dawn felt like punching her. "I can find my own way home. I don't need you."

Grace turned, hands on hips. In an icy voice, she said, "I wouldn't bank on that, sweetheart."

# Chapter
# Ten

PERCHED ON THE edge of her bed, still damp from taking a protracted shower, Dawn rubbed antiseptic cream into a long shallow scratch along one thigh. The injury had happened when she was stumbling through the jungle. It was all that woman's fault. Grace Ramsay. She thought about those hands touching her, the feel of that body heavy and warm, that mouth. How dared she do that? What sort of woman was she?

A lesbian, that's what sort. A woman who has sex with other women. Dawn could hardly bear to contemplate it. Clutching her throbbing temples, she tried desperately to think of anything but Grace Ramsay. Sweat broke across her skin once more, and she shifted uncomfortably. Her body felt unbearably tense, wrenched from within. How could she have let this happen? One minute they were talking like civilized people, and the next minute they were kissing. *Two women!* It hardly seemed real.

Stuffing her hands between her legs, where she was still throbbing, she tumbled back onto her cool sheets. She'd had a lucky escape, she told herself. It could have been worse. At least Grace had stopped when Dawn said no. She remembered a date she'd once had with a man who didn't understand the word 'no.' It had been terrible, frightening. When she told her friends they just shrugged. That type of thing was normal. He was drunk. Next time don't let him in the house. Next time! Dawn shuddered, rejecting the image.

In the void, she could feel Grace's mouth, her skin, hear the bewilderment in her voice. Grace had thought Dawn was a lesbian. How could she? Dawn didn't look anything like a lesbian. She thought about Cody and Annabel, about Grace herself. Did they look like lesbians? They were exceptions, she decided. Any of them could get a man. Apparently, none of them wanted to.

Why not? Had something awful happened to them when they were young, something that had turned them against men forever? Maybe they had been molested. How terrible. Well, that hadn't happened to her. She didn't hate men. She spared a moment's thought for Nigel. No, she didn't even hate Nigel. In fact, she felt...nothing. Absolutely nothing. It was all she'd ever felt, she thought guiltily. Even sex was—she groped for an adequate description—tolerable...predictable...quick. Normal, in other words.

If there were women who had fantastic sex, she didn't know any of them. Thrilling, passionate sex happened in paperbacks, not real life. In real life it was all a bit of a letdown. Five minutes of groping and gasping, then he falls asleep. Give me a cigarette any day, Trish always said. It tastes better. Feels better. Lasts longer and you don't have to feed it.

Revolting, but true. Only... Dawn writhed miserably. She had never experienced anything like the arousal she had felt with Grace. She hadn't known such sensations existed. It was mortifying. Of course there was a logical explanation. She had suffered a trauma. She was on drugs. *And* she had mixed these with alcohol during dinner. Obviously this combination had affected her behavior and impaired her judgment. She was not in full possession of her senses.

None of this was her fault. She hadn't done anything to encourage Grace Ramsay. Quite the opposite. It was Grace who had pestered her, Grace who had obviously planned the whole thing, asking her to a romantic dinner, flirting with her. It was Grace who had kissed her first. Grace knew exactly what she was doing. She probably seduced straight women just for the hell of it.

Dawn chewed her lip, wincing at the sweet salty taste of blood. Damn Grace Ramsay! If she never saw that wretched woman again, it would be too soon.


CURSING DAWN BEAUMONT beneath her breath, Grace slammed her cottage door, strode into the kitchen and hauled a bottle of Cognac out of the pantry. Straight, for God's sake, and broadcasting double messages every time she blinked those baby blue eyes.

For a moment Grace wondered if Dawn was playing games. There were straight women who fooled around with lesbians, but backed off real quick when they couldn't take the heat. Maybe this was how Dawn got her kicks.

Grace was appalled at herself. How could she have misjudged the situation so badly? Why hadn't she taken her time, played it cool? She was so certain Dawn would fall eagerly into her bed, she had blown it. What an amateur.

She poured a double shot and edgily prowled her sitting room. Being turned down so dramatically was something of a novelty, but who needed it? She pictured Dawn, willing and responsive in her arms. The woman had wanted her. Damn it, she was just about coming before Grace had time to get her panties off.

Draining her glass, Grace licked the residue from her lips and gazed out her window. It was time she went home and got laid. She visualized herself cruising babes at the local clubs, picking up some cutie who understood the rules of the game.

Dawn was too damned young, she decided. And implausible as it seemed, maybe she really was a straight girl who had come down with the last shower of rain. Grace shook her head. No. Dawn wasn't straight. Grace had played around with straight women. They were curious, titillated at their own daring, kidding themselves they were doing you some kind of favor.

There had been none of that porn movie plasticity in Dawn, nothing furtive about her kisses, her body's clear signals. She had seemed...inexperienced. Grace toyed with the word and realized it fitted the young Australian perfectly.

It had been so long since she'd had sex with a novice, she had almost forgotten the classic symptoms. She recalled Dawn's tentative hands; her mouth, frozen at first, then responsive; her startled backing off. Dawn had never had sex with a woman. In fact, she hadn't even figured out she was a lesbian.

Grace almost laughed out loud. This put a whole new complexion on things. The Vuitton trunk was not a lost cause after all. Strolling outdoors, she peered into the dark mass of the jungle until she could just make out the dark plane of a cottage roof jutting above the palms.

She could picture Dawn tossing miserably on her bed, wet and unfulfilled, but still trying to convince herself she was heterosexual. Poor, uptight little Dawn—she probably thought there was a law against masturbation, too.

# Chapter
# Eleven


ROBERT B. HAUSMANN was the picture of geniality. He rose, offered his hand, and pulled out a chair with studied ease.

Annabel seated herself and declined a drink. "I don't think this will take long," she said, removing the Argus folder from her satchel and extending it to her companion. "I've read your offer, Mr. Hausmann, and I've given the matter a good deal of thought. But the answer is still no. I'm not selling."

Robert Hausmann settled comfortably into his own chair and accepted the folder without a blink. "I confess I'm disappointed. I had hoped we might do business." He shrugged, steepling his hands. "It's your decision, of course."

*That was it?* Annabel eyed him with suspicion. She had expected at least an attempt to negotiate. "I imagine you have other options."

"I'm the kind of guy who sees every setback as an opportunity." Hausmann's expression was one of calm benevolence. "It's a changing world out there. No more Iron Curtain. The Chinese have canned the little gray pajamas. India has the bomb."

"So you may not proceed with your plans for the South Pacific, after all?"

"Now, Annabel," he chided silkily. "You and I both know what that kind of inside information is worth on the open market."

It was obvious what Hausmann was getting at, Annabel thought. Once news of Argus's plans for Asia/Pacific expansion became public property, stock prices for its local subsidiaries would hit the roof. Anyone who had invested immediately prior to an announcement would make a killing.

Hausmann apparently suspected her of trying to assess the prospects, trying to measure the impact of her decision. She found herself wondering how much stock he'd acquired lately and whether it could be traced to him.

"There are rumors," Hausmann confided. "It's almost

impossible to keep this kind of thing quiet, as you know. We climbed ten points overnight. Of course, making an erroneous assumption about our plans could be disastrous for any big player. And it seems someone is in the market right now..."

"A hostile takeover bid, perhaps?" Annabel speculated sweetly.

The barb went straight home, provoking a thin-lipped smile. "Nothing on that scale." He flicked a dismissive hand. "Between you and me, I've heard it's some bankrupt banana republic taking a flyer."

The words had a chilling deliberation about them. Reading between the lines, Annabel understood why Hausmann radiated confidence. He must have convinced the Cook Islands Premier the deal was on. Annabel wanted to believe a man elected to the highest office in this tiny nation would not gamble government money on an insider share purchase. Hausmann had to be bluffing. Yet, what if he wasn't?

Annabel felt sick. The government was already broke. If the Premier had been suckered into dumping what scant financial reserves they had on some illicit share market punt, the repercussions would be disastrous.

Having delivered this shot across her bow, Hausmann was on his feet. "I wish I could spend more time in your charming company. It's been a real pleasure." Almost as an afterthought, he added, "I gather there's nothing I can offer that could persuade you to change your mind?"

"I have everything I want in life, Mr. Hausmann," Annabel responded coolly. "Selling Moon Island would be a loss, not a gain."

"Well, I'm sorry you feel that way. Very sorry. And I'm sure I won't be the only one." With a reptilian smile, he walked away, leaving Annabel gazing uneasily after him.

A short while later, as she was preparing to leave, a waiter approached and handed her an envelope, explaining that Mr. Hausmann had asked if she would deliver it to one of her guests.

With a jolt, Annabel read the name scrawled across it. Dr. Grace Ramsay.

GRACE SAGGED BACK against a leafy papaya tree and disconsolately sipped from her flask. It was dusk, and she had found no trace of the elusive Night Queen. By the time the first hint of that exotic fragrance wafted into the tropical night, the jungle would be enveloped in darkness, its most tightly held secrets safe once more from prying humanity.

She hoped she could track the plant down before she left. It
was a rare specimen any institution would be pathetically grateful for, exactly the kind of donation that would reap vast public
relations gains for Argus. Visualizing tangible expressions of
Robert Hausmann's gratitude, Grace methodically surveyed the
area around her.

Tomorrow she would conduct one last grid search, she
decided. This would be her last opportunity to procure the
wretched plant. As soon as the island was sold, Argus would
move in with chemical defoliants to make the place more accessi-
ble. Of course, it would not be as pleasant with the dense greenery eliminated, but progress had its price.

Brushing twigs from her legs, Grace wondered whether
Annabel Worth had signed on the dotted line yet. Only a complete fool, or a sentimentalist, would turn down the kind of offer
Argus could make. The Annabel Worth Grace remembered was
neither of those.

Grace marveled at the quirk of fate that had brought her to
the very island Annabel owned. It had come as quite a shock to
arrive in Rarotonga to find her one-time Boston fling waiting to
escort her. If anything, Annabel was even more desirable than
she had been six years ago. Something about her had mellowed
to the point where it was almost impossible to reconcile the laid-
back, sensual Annabel who flew the Moon Island shuttle with
the brittle commodities trader who had once told Grace she
found coffee more satisfying than sex.

Grace had briefly entertained the possibility of a renewed
liaison, but Annabel had quickly made it clear that she was
unavailable. Meeting Cody Stanton, Grace could see why. Annabel and her beloved were obviously joined at the hip, a veritable
billboard for monogamous bliss. Doubtless a commitment ceremony would be the next milestone, then the search for a sperm
donor... Where would it end?

Grace reached a large stand of frangipani flanking Dawn's
cottage and deliberated for a moment on the merits of dropping
in. Maybe Dawn would buy an apology. *Forgive me. I was overcome. You looked so sweet and beautiful in the moonlight. For one
magical moment it would have been easy to believe we were in love. I
wanted just to kiss you, yet when I started I couldn't stop. You were so
warm and willing...*

No, the outraged young Australian would not have a word
of it, Grace guessed. Yet ironically, it was the truth. There had
been a kind of magic about standing beneath the stars with
Dawn, that unworldly scent drifting by, the tropical night laden
with promise. Grace glanced at the cottage and gave a small cyn-

ical laugh. There was something in the Moon Island breeze, she decided, something that softened the brain.

DAWN PACED HER verandah restlessly, thoughts clattering like a toy train on a single track. Again and again, she returned to that disastrous encounter with Grace. She wanted desperately to erase from her consciousness the pressure of Grace's mouth, the warmth of her hands. But the disturbing memories persisted. Hard as she tried, she could find little comfort in the victory of common sense over her new and inexplicable physical urges. Instead of relief at her narrow escape from a lesbian sexual encounter, Dawn felt oddly bereft. Cheated. How humiliating.

Dawn stared up at the moon. It was pale orange, full and alluring against the dark sky. Beyond the palms, the ocean glowed like a black pearl. It was the perfect night for a swim. The very thought made Dawn yearn for the satiny solace of water. Impulsively, she went indoors, gathered up a large towel, and pulled on some sandals.

A narrow track led through a musky entanglement of vines and leaves to the beach. Dawn tossed her walking stick, clothing and shoes into a pile on the sand and lay naked on a towel beneath the starry tapestry of the sky. The beauty of the night was heart-stopping. It was so still—just the throbbing cadence of the ocean and the occasional sigh of the palms in response to a hesitant breeze.

Trickling sand through her fingers, Dawn thought about the huge fish she had released. It was out there somewhere in the milky ocean, swimming free, alive and joyful. She almost wished she could trade places with it. Rolling onto her stomach, she propped her chin on her forearms and stared out to sea.

A dark blob on the ocean's moon-dappled surface drew her attention. It was moving slowly across the bay. She caught a glimpse of arms and froze. A swimmer; some other person in her bay, intruding on her night. Who else could it be but Grace Ramsay? The blob drew closer to the beach. It loomed out of the water, stretched languidly, and shook its head.

Closing her eyes, Dawn tried to block out the sight of that body, lithe and naked, glistening in the moonlight. Grace paused, staring along the beach as though she could sense someone's presence. Dawn held her breath, kept her head low, willed herself not to move a muscle. But when Grace started walking up the beach toward her, panic mobilized her limbs and, scrambling to her feet, she dragged her towel around her and lurched toward the jungle.

"Dawn! Wait!" The voice was shockingly near. "Come on in. The water's incredible."

Dawn's stomach curled. She glanced back over her shoulder. "I didn't mean to disturb you," she said in a voice that barely sounded like her own. Clearing her throat, she added, "I didn't know anyone was here."

Grace halted only when she was so close they were nearly touching. In the moonlight, she glowed marble-smooth, her hollows and contours deeply shadowed. Droplets of water studded her skin like thousands of tiny jewels. "Actually, I was hoping you might show up."

Keeping her eyes above chest level, Dawn wished she could read Grace's expression. But all she could make out was a broad smile, white in the darkness of her face. Her voice held no trace of last night's fury. Was this how they were going to play it—just carry on as if nothing had happened?

"Come on." Grace reached casually for her hand. "Pretend we're friends, okay? I won't bite."

Vacillating, Dawn glanced toward the beckoning sea. She knew she should walk away, proud and defiant, but her legs refused to cooperate. Telling herself that a swim was what she had come down here for, she reluctantly dropped her towel and allowed Grace to lead her along the wet sand toward the deeper part of the lagoon.

"Wonderful night, isn't it?" Grace remarked as they waded into the sea.

Absurdly conscious of their nakedness, Dawn croaked a meaningless response, thankful her burning cheeks wouldn't show in the darkness. The water was warm and infinitely soothing, caressing her scarred thighs like a thousand fingertips. As they moved deeper, Dawn drifted onto her belly, relieved of the aching pressure of standing. Weightless, she kicked away from Grace, and swam in a slow arc around the bay.

There was no need to be apprehensive about being here alone with her neighbor, she reasoned. What had happened last night was a mistake, plain and simple. Obviously Grace wanted to forget about it as much as Dawn did. An apology might have been nice, but Dawn wouldn't hold her breath. After this swim, she would say a polite goodnight and go straight home. Civilized. Responsible. Mature.

Reaching the shallows, she got to her feet. There was no sign of Grace in the moonlit waters, no seal-like head bobbing, no splash of feet.

Dawn gazed around. After a long moment, she called,

"Grace? Where are you?"

The surface broke directly in front of her. "I'm right here."

"You scared me."

"I seem to be making a habit of that."

Wanting to nip the topic in the bud, Dawn said, "Let's just forget about...what happened."

"If that's what you want. I've found it hard to think about anything else."

Dawn's breath jammed her throat like cotton wool. "I should be going." Heart pummeling the walls of her chest, she started to wade ashore.

"Don't go." Grace's voice arrested her. "I'm not bringing it up to embarrass you. Please. I want to say something."

Dawn tucked her shaking hands into her armpits and turned to face the other woman. She didn't want to have this conversation. "There's no need," she said, dropping her eyes. "I know I gave you the wrong impression. I'm sorry."

"You have nothing to apologize for." Grace closed the distance between them. "I'm sorry for the things I said to you. I was hoping we could maybe start again."

Dawn told herself to leave, leave now. Start again? Grace made it sound so easy. So tempting. "I...can't." Even to her own ears, the protest sounded feeble.

With slow deliberation, Grace touched Dawn's shoulder, her thumb brushing the hollow at the base of her neck. Dawn's immediate urge was to back away, but her feet seemed embedded in the sand. For a long moment, the pounding of her heart in her ears drowned out all other sound—her own voice, the hollow thunder of waves against the reef.

Drawing closer, Grace said, "We could pretend we just met, but by some magic we know each other well." She lowered her mouth to the base of Dawn's throat, where the skin was hotly imprinted with her thumb. Planting a single lingering kiss, she glanced up at Dawn, in unspoken question.

Dawn took a shaky breath. Now was the time to put a stop to this, yet she could not.

Grace took Dawn's face between her hands, kissing her delicately, on the forehead, the eyelids, the cheeks. "Don't be scared," she murmured. "I know this is new for you. If you want me to stop, I will."

Dawn's senses were clamoring. She could feel Grace's breath on her face, feel her own moisture trickling down her thighs to merge with the salt water, the hot ache between her legs. In that moment, Dawn knew she wanted what Grace was offering. She wanted it more than she'd ever wanted anything in her life.

"Just let it happen," Grace whispered against her lips, and this time Dawn's mouth parted and her outstretched fingers met Grace's flesh.

Trembling, she swayed closer. Their breasts slid across one another, nipples as hard as pebbles. Grace's mouth was on her neck, then her shoulders. Her tongue trailed slowly downward to capture the salty rivulets converging between Dawn's breasts. Their stomachs brushed. Grace took her hips and Dawn felt the new and shocking sensation of another woman's sex pressed into hers. She stiffened for a split second, then Grace's arms gathered her close, keeping her safe.

Slipping her hand into Grace's, she allowed herself to be guided from the water. Once on the beach, they clung together in tight embrace, returning kiss for kiss. Dawn dragged her fingers along the curve of Grace's spine, awed by the texture of her flesh, the sinuous outline of her muscles. She rested her hands in the small of Grace's back, then moved on to the wonderful firmness of her ass.

They sank down onto the wet sand, breasts crushed, thighs entwined. Gentle surf fingered its way up the sand to bubble and lap across their legs. Cradling Dawn's head, Grace slid her tongue delicately between her lips, demanding only her compliance. Unresisting, Dawn yielded to exquisite sensation, surrendering herself to Grace's soul-stealing kisses, craving so much more.

Breathing hard, Grace cupped Dawn's face. "Look at me," she commanded, and when Dawn opened her eyes, said huskily, "I want to make love to you. Do you want that?"

Caught between desire and self-doubt, Dawn could not answer for a moment. Eventually, she whispered, "Yes." Realizing she sounded uncertain, she added self-consciously, "I don't know what to do."

Grace's arms closed around her. Smiling, she said, "Yes, you do." She helped Dawn to her feet, cupping seawater to wash the sand off each of them.

Taking Dawn's hand, she led her up the beach to a pile of clothing, shook out a huge towel and drew her down onto the warm soft cotton. Caressing Dawn in long sensual strokes that extended from her breasts to the parting of her thighs, she said, "Tell me you want me." Her mouth was just a breath from Dawn's, their lips almost brushing.

Dawn slid her arms around Grace, wanting to close the distance between them. "I want you," she said thickly.

Grace moved over her, blotting out the moon, erasing the pulse of the ocean, the salt sea smell, until Dawn could feel only her, taste only her, breathe only her. She gasped as Grace slid a thigh between her legs, pressing into Dawn with a sensual determination that made Dawn whimper with shock and pleasure. She clung to Grace, grounding herself in the feel and smell of her. Arching her back, she lifted her hips to increase the relentless pressure, and the two women rocked against one another.

Just when Dawn thought she could bear no more, Grace changed position, sliding an arm beneath Dawn's hips, trailing warm kisses across her stomach and over her thighs until finally centering on the ache between them. Hardly daring to breath, Dawn felt Grace's fingers part her swollen flesh, her tongue soothing and teasing at the same time.

Unbearable heat spread through Dawn's pelvis. Moisture broke across her skin. She cried out as Grace dipped a finger inside her, gradually opening her, working in deeper. Centered where they were most exquisite, the sensations multiplied until Dawn's body was rising and falling, fiercely concentrated on this sensual rite. Reaching down, she dug her fingers into Grace's shoulders, bracing herself.

Grace responded by increasing the pressure of her tongue and the rhythm of her strokes. Lifting her hips in unison, Dawn ached for release from a sharp, unbearable tension that seemed to seize every limb. Overwhelmed, muscles quivering uncontrollably, she felt herself clench around Grace's fingers in a series of tiny, profound spasms. Then she was crying, rocked against the safety of Grace's shoulder, Grace's soft voice repeating, "It's all right, baby. It's all right."

# Chapter
# Twelve


WHEN DAWN AWOKE, she was alone. The clock beside Grace's bed said noon. She had slept for hours, a deep, satisfying sleep. Eyes closed, she recaptured for a moment the sensations of the night, then stretched languidly, kicking away the sheets, and bathing in the breeze that seeped through the window.

Somewhere on the outer reaches of her consciousness, she could make out the sounds of another person moving about in the cottage, footfalls, the occasional thud or clatter. A hot-water kettle whistled; a woman was humming. On a hook behind Grace's door were a couple of brightly colored sarongs. Knotting one of these to cover her breasts, Dawn pushed her tangled hair off her face and ventured out in the direction of the noises.

Grace was at the small table in the kitchen, pouring a cup of tea. As Dawn hovered in the doorway, she glanced up, smiling broadly. Dawn flushed. She didn't want to, but the sight of Grace in her white shirt and khaki shorts, her eyes dark and knowing, made her feel self-conscious and exposed. What must Grace think of her, she wondered.

"Sleep well?" Grace asked. She didn't seem embarrassed or jumpy.

Murmuring some inconsequential response, Dawn found herself fascinated by Grace's slender, purposeful hands as they poured tea, buttered a roll. She quickly lowered her head, certain her graphic memories of those hands were written all over her face.

"I was hoping you'd wake before I go," Grace said nonchalantly.

Dawn looked up. "Go? Where are you going?"

"I'm borrowing Cody's boat for the afternoon to do some depth-testing out near the reef."

"I see." Inching her way into the room, Dawn sat down at the table. Why did she feel dejected all of a sudden? Grace was simply carrying on life as usual. What had she expected? "When will you be back?" The words were out before she could prevent them and Dawn felt a rush of irritation at herself.

Grace shrugged. "It's hard to say." Her expression became slightly guarded. "What are your plans for the day?"

"Nothing in particular."

"You could come with me if you want." The invitation sounded hesitant.

She was offering out of politeness. Dawn quickly shook her head. "No. No thanks. I'll give it a miss."

Grace's glance became intent. "Are you upset about last night?"

Upset? Dawn struggled with the question. No, that didn't begin to describe how she was feeling. Devastated was more like it. Stunned. Overwhelmed. She felt as though she had stumbled into an emotional maze and would never find her way back to the person she had been.

Grace must have interpreted her silence as embarrassment, for she said, "We don't have to talk about it if you'd rather not. Last night never happened, okay?"

Dawn stared at the floor. Grace might be able to dismiss what they'd done, but she certainly couldn't.

"Suits me fine," Grace was assuring her, and this time Dawn detected a harder note. "Honestly. I had a good time, and I think you did, too. Let's just leave it at that. No strings attached, okay?"

Dawn's throat felt swollen. "Okay," she croaked. Liar! her mind shouted. She wanted to get up, throw her arms around Grace, beg her not to go. She wanted them to lie naked in the truth of daylight and make love all over again. But Grace was getting to her feet, brushing off her shorts, glancing at her watch. Clearly this was just a morning like any other morning for her. Maybe she did this kind of thing all the time.

Dawn folded her arms across her breasts. Hungry butterflies chewed a wayward path from the pit of her stomach to the cleft between her legs. "Well, I'll be going then," she said in a high brittle voice. "I've got some letters to write."

Grace gave her another piercing look. "Dawn—" she began, then seemed to reconsider, her mouth wry. "You don't have to rush off," she said in a neutral tone. "Help yourself to breakfast."

Averting her eyes, Dawn muttered an inaudible thank you. Breakfast. Only minutes ago she had been starving but now the very thought of food made her nauseous.

Grace was suddenly so close their bodies were brushing. "Are you really okay? I mean, I'll wait and walk you home, of course."

Dawn was tempted to spill out all her feelings, but something in Grace's eyes prevented her. There was an unmistakable reserve, a distance that tore at Dawn's heart. Grace didn't really want to hear what she was feeling, Dawn realized with sharp dismay. Tongue-tied, she turned her attention toward the empty cups on the table and started gathering them up. "Nothing's wrong," she said, forcing indifference. "I can get myself home. Have fun on the boat."

Meeting Grace's eyes, she caught a quick, shuttered glimpse of relief. Then Grace was twisting her earring, her face relaxing into a lopsided grin.

"Later then." Blowing Dawn a kiss, she sauntered from the room, apparently without a care in the world.


IN THE TORPID swill of late afternoon, Annabel's clothes were glued to her body. Trying to straighten herself up, she removed her damp shirt, shook it out, and donned it again. With a mixture of emotions, she knocked on Grace's door-frame and waited. Six years had passed since they were lovers, and it had been a shock to see Grace after so long. She'd been on the island for nearly three weeks, and Annabel had done her level best to avoid her. She felt an occasional pang of guilt for keeping her distance, only because it seemed immature somehow.

She had nothing to hide. She had told Cody about Grace, emphasizing the fact that their relationship was never serious. They had hooked up if they happened to be visiting their respective cities on business. Their contact comprised nothing more than a series of convenient sexual encounters. Annabel knew Cody had difficulty understanding. She was such a straightforward person. Why have casual sex when you could have a full-time lover and genuine romance? It was as simple as that.

There was no answer from inside the cottage. Dropping into one of the cane verandah chairs, Annabel contemplated the gardens around her. It had been a massive job to restore them after Hurricane Mary, but these days it was difficult to tell that this part of the island had been so badly ravaged.

In the tropics everything grew fast, fleshy and fecund. The pulse of the jungle was sluggish at this time of day. In an hour or so, a frenetic burst of energy would send it rocketing, as myriad creatures sought their last meal of the day and headed for home. Annabel could relate. Whenever she was away, she experienced the same powerful drive to return home, picturing Cody on the verandah immersed in some paperback, herself pottering in the kitchen.

Briefly she wallowed in private delight. She wouldn't swap this life for anything, least of all a bloated bank balance and a pile of scrip. It's not like she and Cody needed the money. When Annabel inherited Moon Island from her aunt three years earlier, she had also inherited a substantial fortune.

For a long while, she had left the money untouched, feeling oddly guilty about having it. But recently, at Cody's suggestion, she had formed a charitable trust. With wealth it was possible to make a difference in the world, for good or for ill. What a pity so many powerful people and businesses chose the latter, she thought.

Glancing at the letter she had set down on the small wicker table nearby, she wondered why Robert B. Hausmann was writing to Grace. What exactly had Grace said about her research work on the island? Something obscure to do with coral reef formations. Annabel hadn't paid much attention at the time. She was too busy trying to sort out her feelings about having a piece of her past return to haunt her.

Had Grace mentioned for whom she was working? No. Had she concealed it deliberately? Annabel frowned. Somewhere in the back of her mind a nasty little doubt hovered, reminding her that Grace was an opportunist from way back. She hadn't let ethics stand in her way in the past, and from the inviting look she'd given Annabel right under Cody's nose, that clearly hadn't changed.

"Annabel!" a voice hailed her.

Grace emerged from a thicket of vines. She looked surprised and pleased. Despite herself, Annabel found her pulse responding to those bold, assessing eyes.

"It's good to see you," Grace said. She paused, hands on hips, catching her breath.

Watching the rise and fall of her breasts, Annabel allowed herself to remember that body. She felt oddly detached. Grace Ramsay was one of the most exciting lovers she had ever had. It was strange to see her now and feel aware of the sexual pull that had first drawn them together, yet be unmoved by it. "I have something for you, Grace," she said. "From Robert Hausmann."

Grace looked briefly startled, then an untroubled calm descended on her features, and she took the envelope, sliding it casually into her shorts pocket.

"You're acquainted with Mr. Hausmann?" Annabel asked. Grace's eyes were calculating. Annabel could almost hear her weighing up her options, trying to guess how much Annabel actually knew. "Don't even think about lying to me, Grace," she challenged coldly. "We know each other better than that."

For a moment there was a hint of defiance in Grace's expression, then she shrugged. "I'm employed by Argus. I can't say I know Robert Hausmann personally. We've met, that's all."

"What are you doing here?"

"Some research."

"For Argus?"

"That's right."

"Did you know Argus wants to buy the island from me?"

Grace hesitated. "I gathered so. We need a base in the Pacific. Housing for staff...that kind of thing."

It sounded glib. "So you're here for three weeks to find out whether the island is habitable? Stretches credibility, Grace."

"That's not my problem. I'm just doing my job."

"I want to see your report," Annabel demanded.

Grace jerked upright. "Absolutely not. That report is confidential."

"As from today that report is totally irrelevant," Annabel tossed back. "I've turned down your boss's offer to buy the island."

Grace looked briefly uncertain, then said, "That makes no difference. Argus commissioned a report from me, and I'll deliver it. If you want to see it, you'd better speak to Mr. Hausmann."

Annabel took a deep breath. Grace was hiding something. Everything about her shouted it. She looked cagey, defensive. "Grace, please." Annabel pressed her. "What is Argus really doing out here? I can't swallow some line about office premises in the middle of nowhere."

Grace fell silent. Her eyes glinted with appreciation. "You know," she drawled, "being in love has done wonders for your sex appeal, Annabel."

"Grace! I'm asking you a question."

"Give me a break. You know I can't answer that."

"The word is won't, not can't. Look, Grace, this is my home. I have a right to know what some huge conglomerate is doing sniffing around here."

"You're asking me to place my professional reputation at risk...to breach confidentiality."

"I don't remember ethics being a problem for you before."

"Spare me the guilt trip, Annabel. You're no saint. You were still with Claire when you went to bed with me."

"You know damned well Claire and I were breaking up. I was depressed and unhappy."

"You were horny."

Annabel took a sharp breath. "And you were still living with

Carol."

"So what? She knew I saw other women."

"She knew you weren't capable of being committed, you mean!"

"I don't have to listen to this." Grace stalked into the cottage, Annabel marching after her. "I can't see why you're so damned obsessed with my report. You're not selling the island anyway, so what the hell does it matter to you?"

"I want to know what Argus is up to. Don't worry," she added with deep cynicism. "I won't advertise it. Your ass will be covered." Annabel met Grace's eyes levelly. "It matters because I care about these islands and the people who live here. I wouldn't expect you to understand."

"Why? Because I'm a slut?" Grace's tone was flippant.

Aggravated, Annabel said, "I'm sure it must make life simpler not to give a damn about anybody except yourself. But some of us actually care. Some of us don't want to turn our backs on the wider ramifications of what we do."

"Christ!" Grace slammed a hand down on the kitchen counter. "When did you become so fucking self-righteous?"

"When did you become so fucking alienated?" Annabel hurled back.

She was surprised to see dull red blossom in Grace's cheeks. There was an odd vulnerability about her, all of a sudden. Understanding that she had struck a nerve, Annabel said, "I'm sorry. That was uncalled for."

Grace's gaze fell to some papers sitting on the desk in the adjoining room. Breathing hard, her mouth tight with anger, she stalked over to it, snatched up a thick document and thrust it at Annabel, saying, "Here. Satisfied?"

Annabel sat down and began skimming the scientific text. After a few minutes, she lifted her head. "I can't believe you're involved in this."

Grace stared at her, hard-eyed. "What's the crime exactly? I'm an environmental geologist. This is what I do."

"You're talking about exploding half the reef around the island, about incinerating toxic chemicals and burying the waste. Razing the vegetation, destroying the habitat of every creature on the island." Annabel was shaking. "This is sickening. I can't believe it."

"Oh, for God's sake, Annabel. Where've you been all your life? We produce five hundred million tons of hazardous waste a year, back home. Where do you think it all goes? Rich countries don't deal with their own shit. They pay poor countries to bury it in their backyards. Didn't you know that?"

Annabel cradled her head in her hands. If Argus didn't get Moon Island, they were bound to find an alternative. Maybe the government would offer one of the more remote atolls. The Cook Islands could become another Marshalls, people dying slowly and mysteriously from the effects of windborne contamination.

"Grace, how can you do this?" A sob worked its way into Annabel's throat. "How can you work for these people? This is global depravity dressed up as commercial pragmatism."

"Argus is a responsible company in a difficult industry," Grace said coldly. "They value my skills. What do you expect me to do? Martyr myself to some poverty-stricken, ecologically sound bunch of do-gooders?"

"I don't expect anything of you." Annabel could hear her own bitterness. "I can't believe you stayed here doing this behind my back. How could you be so dishonest? We were lovers!"

"We were fucking," Grace hissed. "That's all. Spare me the guilt trip, for chrissakes. We can't all afford to wallow in high-blown ethics. Some of us have to work for a living. It so happens my career is important to me. In fact, it's the most important thing in the world."

Annabel felt a rush of sadness. The Grace she remembered hadn't been this hard. What on earth had happened to make her so callous? "If that's true, then I can only feel sorry for you."

"Don't torture yourself," Grace retorted. "I'm perfectly happy."

"I'm going now." Annabel dropped the report disgustedly on the table. "I'd like you to leave the island. You can come with me to Raro the day after tomorrow."

"Suits me," Grace said without emotion. "I'm done here anyway."

They walked outdoors and stood side by side on the verandah for a long moment, gazing out at the amethyst twilight. Eventually Annabel said very quietly, "I'm sorry things turned out like this." Turning, she caught a glimpse of pain in Grace's eyes and impulsively touched her arm. "Grace, what happened to you? "

Grace's expression was glazed. "Isn't it obvious? Life happened. I got older and wiser."

"I haven't forgotten absolutely everything about you," Annabel said in a dry tone. "You were never so..." She groped for a word.

"Ruthless?" Grace suggested.

"I'm not sure I'd go that far. But okay." Annabel smiled faintly. "Want to talk about it?"

Grace hesitated. She looked numb. "I don't know if I can."

"Maybe it's time you found out." Annabel slipped an arm around Grace's waist. "Humor me. Pretend we're strangers on a train."


THE SUN WAS low and orange when Dawn decided she couldn't stand another moment of dithering around in Frangipani Cottage, obsessing over Grace Ramsay. Donning a light sweater and jeans, she hobbled resolutely into the jungle and along the narrow track to Grace's cottage.

Where was her pride, she thought unhappily. Wasn't it enough that she'd gone to bed with a virtual stranger, without it being a woman and without going back for seconds? For that was what she was doing. She couldn't pretend she was seeking Grace out for intellectual stimulation or pleasant company on a long tropical night. No. She wanted to have sex with her.

The admission was so shocking that Dawn stopped in her tracks, the squashy nighttime sounds of the jungle providing a lurid backdrop to her thoughts. She was hot and throbbing between her legs, empty where she wanted to be full. She started walking again.

Creepers caught at her hair and her hands felt damp and sticky from grappling with the tangled vegetation. Darkness was falling swiftly, and for a moment she was frightened she would never find her way to the other cottage. Then she caught the sound of music, melodious but slightly tinny. Grace's battery-operated CD player.

An involuntary smile tugged at the corners of her mouth. She would never be able to hear that particular Annie Lennox recording without remembering that first night with Grace. But there was something else. Voices. She peered between the huge leaves of a papaya.

They were standing on the verandah, Grace and another woman she couldn't quite see. Dawn debated whether to continue on. She told herself she was being stupid. Even if Grace did have a visitor, they wouldn't mind Dawn showing up. But somehow it wasn't the same. She didn't want to arrive at Grace's cottage as an uninvited third party. That wasn't the mental picture she'd fabricated: Grace surprised and delighted to see her, the two of them melting into one another's arms.

Crestfallen, she contemplated the women on the verandah. She should never have come, she thought dismally. She was behaving like a lovesick adolescent. Her eyes stung and she balled her fists against them. How could this have happened to her? It was some kind of divine retribution, she decided, the inevitable consequences of tempting fate, her punishment for thinking the things she had about women like Cody and Annabel...lesbians.

Now she'd had an affair with one of them, even if it had only lasted one night. And here she was, the very next day, hanging out for more.

Numbly, she focused on the two women. They appeared to be deep in conversation, heads close together. With a shock, she recognized Annabel Worth. Her arm was over Grace's shoulder. They moved together, holding one another in a prolonged embrace.

Dawn jerked her head away. She couldn't bear to see any more. Blindly, she stumbled back into the night. Grace and Annabel! She felt like throwing up. How could they?

# Chapter
# Thirteen

"TIRED, HONEY?" CODY bent over Annabel and planted a kiss on her forehead. Annabel had seemed oddly preoccupied ever since she got home from Rarotonga the day before.

"I'm sorry, darling." Annabel looked up. "I'm not exactly good company this morning, am I?"

Cody occupied the sofa next to her lover. Sliding her arms loosely around Annabel's neck, she nuzzled her pale cheek. "We could work on that."

Annabel lifted a hand to Cody's hair, absently stroking it. "I love you," she murmured.

"I love you, too." Cody observed Annabel's frown with a twinge of apprehension. "Is something wrong? Did something happen at the meeting?"

Annabel hesitated. Wearily, she said, "Grace is working for Argus, the company trying to buy the island. She's been writing a report on how to turn Moon Island into a toxic waste dump."

"You're kidding me." Cody was aghast. "Toxic waste! Are they crazy?"

"It's a big business. Companies pay Argus millions of dollars to deal with their disposal problem. Argus exports the waste to third world countries willing to accept it for a fee."

"Are you saying the Cook Islands government would allow this? I mean, even if we sold Moon Island to these scumbags, surely they'd never be allowed to bring that kind of stuff here."

"Money talks. I got the impression Hausmann has cut some kind of deal with the Premier."

"I don't believe it!"

"It gets worse," Annabel said. "I have a feeling the Premier might have used government money to buy shares in Argus' Pacific subsidiary. So if the deal doesn't go through and the share price falls—"

"Curtains for the government." Cody got the picture right away. "So this Hausmann guy thinks he can blackmail us over that?"

"He didn't spell it out in so many words."

"And your pal Grace works for this asshole." Cody shook her head. "That lousy, two-faced..." She trailed off. You weren't supposed to call your lover's ex a rotten bitch.

Annabel made a helpless gesture. "I've found this a low-wattage experience, too."

"What are we going to do?" Cody asked.

"It's already done. I've told Hausmann we're not selling. Let's just hope he was bluffing about the government buying stock."

"And Grace?" Cody wanted to escort her off the island personally.

"She's leaving. I'm taking her to Raro tomorrow."

"This is why you went to see her last night?" Cody had felt uneasy about that. She should have known Annabel wouldn't have gone calling on her one-time fling without good reason.

"I gave her a hard time," Annabel said. "I feel kind of lousy about it now."

"You feel lousy!" Cody snorted. "You're not the one who just accepted women's hospitality and snuck around behind their backs arranging to destroy their island."

"Don't think too badly of her, sweetheart. Grace has some problems."

Cody bit back a sharp comment. If Annabel wanted to defend her ex's disgraceful behavior, that was up to her. It must be hard to admit you'd slept with such a jerk, even if it was only casual. She took Annabel's hand. "Well, as far as I'm concerned Grace can go fuck herself. I'm glad it's all over with these Argus people."

"Me, too," Annabel said. Her voice was flat and controlled, but there was an edge of emotion. Annabel sounded worried.

Trying to ignore the shiver that crept along her spine, Cody kissed her cheek softly. "It is over, isn't it?" she persisted.

"I'm not sure." Annabel gazed out the window. "I guess I was expecting Hausmann to put up more of a fight when I turned him down. The guy has a reputation for getting his own way."

"What does that mean?"

"He plays to win. But this time he backed down like a lamb. It struck me as odd. That's all."

Cody shrugged. "Well, maybe he was just trying his luck. Now that he knows we're never going to be interested, he'll just have to find some other place to set up shop." She stroked Annabel's hair. "Don't worry about it, darling. No one's going to take the island away from us."

"Sometimes I get frightened," Annabel said in a muffled voice. "It almost feels too good to be true... that I have you and we live in this beautiful place. I'm scared that one day I'll wake up and find it was all a dream."

Drawing Annabel into her arms, Cody kissed her passionately. "Did that feel real?"

Returning her kisses with an urgency that verged on desperation, Annabel whispered, "I love you so very much." She drew back suddenly, eyes intense. "Promise me something," she said, gripping Cody's shoulders. "If anything ever happens to me, you won't give up the island."

"Annabel!" A ripple of fright made the hairs on Cody's nape stand up. "What are you talking about?"

"Just promise me," Annabel insisted.

Cody stared at the woman she loved. "I promise," she said, filled with churning unease.

DAWN WAS ON her verandah when Grace sauntered into view, tall and tanned and heart-stopping. The mere sight of her made Dawn perspire. How could any woman be so blatantly, effortlessly sexual? And how could Grace look so relaxed and unguarded when she was having an affair with Annabel Worth? They were ratting on Cody. No doubt they imagined she would never guess. Well, Dawn had other plans.

Climbing the verandah steps, Grace offered an insolent half-smile. "God, I'd kill for an iced tea," she said.

Dawn gave her a frosty look. "Help yourself. You know where the kitchen is."

Grace didn't seem to notice the chilly reception. Tossing her hat down onto a chair, she cast Dawn a glance that was pointedly flirtatious. "Want anything?"

*Only to slap that grin off your face.* Controlling her voice, Dawn said, "No thanks."

Grace returned with a large glass of iced tea and sat in the chair next to Dawn's. She stretched out her legs, kicking off her sandals with an arrogant familiarity that rattled Dawn more than she could believe. How dare she! How dare she come bowling in, all innocence, when she was carrying on with another woman—a woman who was already in a relationship, no less.

Dawn didn't realize she was glaring until Grace tilted her head and those granite eyes flashed knowingly. "Are you mad at me, Dawn?"

"No. Why should I be?"

"Why indeed?" Grace sipped her drink, her gaze firmly riveted to Dawn's face. "Are you annoyed that I didn't come over last night?"

"No doubt you had better things to do," Dawn said stonily.

"I get the feeling you're trying to tell me something. What is it?"

Dawn shrugged. She felt out of her depth. What right did she have to demand explanations from Grace about her behavior? They'd spent a night together. So what? Did she own Grace now?

Wiping her hands across her T-shirt, she tried not to notice the smooth length of Grace's thighs, the lines of her lean disciplined body, the faint sharp smell of cloves. Her attention drifted to the parting of Grace's shirt, the press of those toffee-tinted nipples, the shadow of her breasts.

She wanted her. She wanted her so desperately, she could see herself on her knees, begging, *please fuck me*. Self-disgust made her look away. How could she even think that? What had she become—a slave to some previously unsuspected carnality?

Grace was a liar and a home-wrecker, Dawn reminded herself brutally. But her body cried, *who cares?* All she wanted was to lie naked with her and wallow once more in mindless pleasure. What a slut.

"I'm leaving the island tomorrow," Grace said quietly. "I've come to say goodbye."

"Goodbye?" Dawn heard herself echo. "You're not coming back?"

"My work's finished." There was a newer, harder note. "So, I'm flying out with Annabel in the afternoon and heading back home on the first flight I can get."

*With Annabel.* Dawn tried not to react.

"I just wanted to tell you." Grace fidgeted with her diamond earring. "I enjoyed spending time with you."

This was it, Dawn thought bitterly. *Thanks for the sex, sweetheart. See you later. Later, as in never.* Her fingers dug into her palms, making tight little fists. She felt like punching Grace in the teeth. Instead she jerked to her feet and on the most offhand note she could muster, said, "Well I'll be seeing you then."

Turning away from Grace, she stared out to sea. She would not cry in front of this woman. Grace Ramsay could rot in hell, as far as she was concerned.

"Dawn." A hand touched her shoulder. "We don't have to do it this way. You're angry at me, and I don't even know why." Grace turned Dawn slowly around, sliding her arms loosely around her waist.

Dawn felt her eyes drawn inexorably to Grace's. She

watched the pupils dilate, the thick straight lashes droop with sleepy sensuality. Her lips parted to frame a sentence telling Grace exactly what she thought of her, but the words never came. Instead something tangible and shockingly lusty passed between them, and Dawn lifted her fingers to Grace's mouth. It was soft, a little dry. She bent forward, moistened it with her tongue. It parted invitingly.

The kiss deepened. Hands shaking, Dawn twisted Grace's shirt roughly from her shorts.

Grace laughed softly. "What's the rush?" Her hands moved to Dawn's hips, pulling her close, so they were hard against one another. Her eyes were full of wicked intent. "You want me, Dawn?"

A gush of liquid soaked Dawn's panties. Grace stole one of her hands, kissed the scars across its knuckles, then guided it between her tanned thighs, sliding it back and forth across the damp seam that parted the flesh Dawn remembered so well. Her mouth was on Dawn's neck, hot and insistent. Dawn increased the pressure of her fingers against Grace, irked at the fabric barrier that denied them their destination. She tugged at Grace's shorts, gasping as Grace's hands found their way beneath her shirt, to pinch and tease her nipples.

"You've made me all wet," Grace whispered in her ear. "What are you going to do about it?"

Breathing hard, Dawn seized one of Grace's hands and pulled her into the cottage. She wanted her so badly, she felt sick. Once in her bedroom, she pushed Grace onto her bed and fell on top of her, tugging clumsily at her clothes. Laughing, Grace took over, deftly removing the offending garments. As Dawn reached for her, Grace quickly changed position, rolling Dawn onto her back and pinning her shoulders down. "You'll just have to wait," she said hoarsely. "I want you first."

She slid first one knee, then the other, between Dawn's thighs and lowered herself over Dawn, kissing her passionately. As the strength fled Dawn's limbs, Grace altered the intensity of her kiss. Slowly, sensually, she moved her mouth over Dawn's cheek, to her ear. In it, she whispered, "You know this is what I came here for, don't you?"

Enjoying Dawn's shivering response, Grace progressed down the column of her neck in a trail of hot kisses. Finally she bit down softly, and again harder, watching the mark of her teeth bloom.

Oddly, she desired Dawn much more than she had on the beach two nights before. That conscious seduction had been fun, hot, good for the ego. Grace was honest enough to admit she

sought the sense of power her casual sexual encounters provided. The interlude with Dawn was no exception, yet Grace had
felt strangely unsettled ever since.

She had not planned to come and say goodbye in person,
instead convincing herself a courteous note would do the trick.
But she was unable to get Dawn off her mind. Right now, she
wanted nothing more than to give her pleasure, to feel that soft,
feminine body yielding in her arms, to gaze down into those
trusting blue eyes and watch the woman in Dawn awakening
with every new sensation.

Grace wound her fingers into Dawn's honey gilt hair and for
a sweet moment, allowed herself to lie on her, resting between
her breasts, listening to the urgent beat of her heart. In a different world, in a different life, she could almost be content with
this, she thought, breathing in the warm, ripeness of Dawn's
body. But this was *her* life, and, on any plane but the physical,
she had nothing to offer any woman.

Adjusting her weight, she leaned on an elbow so her face
was once more above Dawn's. Tenderly, she kissed her, trailing a
hand down the body she was just coming to know. Dawn's
mouth was warm and responsive. Moving against Grace, her fingers digging into the muscles of Grace's back, she returned the
tender kiss with a sensuous demand for more.

Grace pushed a thigh between Dawn's legs, applying just
enough pressure to make Dawn lift her hips and push back. A
primal hunger took possession of Grace and she deepened their
kiss, burying her tongue and changing position so she was completely between Dawn's legs, her weight spreading them wide.
Sliding a hand between their bodies, she entered Dawn hard.
Slippery and swollen, the silken flesh enfolded her fingers.

Stifling Dawn's gasps with her mouth, Grace slid slowly in
and out, guided by the younger woman's cues, the rise of her
hips, the pace of her breathing. Finally breaking their kiss, Dawn
gulped air like it was water. Her eyes shone bright with desire,
the pupils dilated. Rosy color suffused her face and neck. Lost in
arousal, she murmured, "Deeper."

Changing position, Grace knelt astride one of Dawn's thighs
and slid an arm beneath her waist to cradle her. By careful
degrees, she worked a third finger inside, using her thumb
against Dawn's clit. Gloved and saturated within the hot, welcoming passage, Grace's fingers radiated sensation back through
her hand, informing every movement. Suppressing an over-
whelming urge to take Dawn fiercely, she concentrated instead
on learning the idiom of her body.

"You're perfect," she said, aware of a strange shift in her

own emotions. Dawn's surrender was so unreserved, her giving of herself so complete, Grace felt hopelessly moved. Angling her hand for greater depth, she lost herself in their sweet union. Dawn's body felt like home.

Supplicant in Grace's arms, Dawn could not speak. She had never felt so completely exposed. Engulfed by a steadily mounting torrent of sensation, she was frightened. For a split second, she wanted to stop. But it was too late. From deep in her womb, a series of spasms radiated through her body, melting flesh and bone, until Dawn could no longer distinguish Grace's hand from the walls that sheathed it.

Barely opening her eyes, she lifted a hand to Grace's face. The skin was wet. Dawn slid her fingers into the copper hair and drew Grace's head to her belly. For a long while, they remained locked together, blanketed in a calm that transcended all thought. When Grace eventually withdrew her hand, Dawn could still feel its impression within. Smiling, she fell asleep.

HOURS LATER, LYING against Grace's shoulder, Dawn listened to the steady beat of her heart. She allowed a hand to drift across Grace's small taut breasts, the flat plane of her stomach, the springy mat of dark hair below. Their bodies were so different. She stroked her own full heavy breasts, her rounded belly, the soft straight hair between her legs.

Her body felt brand new, her senses sharpened. It was as if she were suddenly attuned to frequency she had not known existed. Grace knew exactly how to touch her. She must have made love with dozens of women, Dawn thought with a pang. Probably gorgeous, clever women who were fantastically accomplished in bed.

*I will never be able to look at women the same way again,* Dawn realized, uncertain whether she was appalled or thrilled by this. In fact, nothing would ever be the same. Turning her face into Grace's breast, she inhaled the saltiness of her skin, grazed her tongue over the soft nipple, slid an arm around her waist. Grace stirred slightly. With a curious sadness, Dawn tightened her embrace.

For the first time in her life she found herself wondering who she really was. It was not something she ever thought about. She had always taken her identity for granted. Dawn Beaumont—champion swimmer, nice girl, respectable family. Her parents were decent, traditional people. Her father was a good provider. Her mother was always there, mostly in the kitchen. They had worked hard to send her to the right schools, to pay for the best swimming coach in Sydney. They were terribly proud of her. What a daughter, her father often said, what a blessing from the Lord.

Her parents were religious—not fanatical, just plodding Protestant churchgoers. They blessed meals, read the Bible on Sundays, and told Dawn to keep herself pure for her future husband. She had ignored them, of course. Dawn figured they knew she had slept with a couple of men. No doubt they settled for thanking God their daughter had avoided getting a disease, or worse, an unwanted pregnancy.

Easing out of Grace's arms, she rolled onto her side and stared at the wall. What would they think of this? Sex with men was tolerated because it would lead to a husband and children. But with a woman? She would never be able to tell them. Well, she might not have to. She'd only done it once... twice. So what? That didn't mean she would want to go to bed with every woman she saw.

Dawn tried to think about something else, but the idea chased her relentlessly. She wanted to sleep with a woman again, she admitted deep in her heart. What did that mean? The question fluttered and danced in her consciousness until she drifted back into sleep, finally surrendering to the answer. *I'm a lesbian.*

# Chapter
Fourteen

A VEIL OF wan light covered the sky and the watery moon retreated as day broke on the island. Alone on Dawn's verandah, Grace sipped her tea and thought about the woman asleep inside.

One Louis Vuitton trunk coming up, she congratulated herself. The prospect fell oddly flat; in fact, it made her downright uneasy. Her skin still tingled with the memory of Dawn. She'd felt so good, so new and fresh. Grace wanted to pleasure her, to indulge her, to open her and get inside. There was something very alluring about Dawn, about her tentative caresses, her naive astonishment at her own physicality.

Subdued, Grace leaned against the balustrade and rubbed the nape of her neck, where tension corded her muscles. She had to go soon. Cody was probably in the motorboat already, chugging around the island on her way to collect their unwelcome guest. Annabel would be waiting at the landing strip, tinkering with that dog of a plane.

With a sinking feeling in the pit of her stomach, Grace scanned the lush surroundings. She hadn't realized how quickly she'd come to take the island for granted. The enormity of Argus's project struck her like a physical blow. Until now, the ultimate plan had seemed distant and unreal, clouded by statistics and calculations. The job was just another handsomely paid contract.

Grace cupped her forehead in her hands. How could she calmly recommend the blasting of a coral reef that was home to thousands of creatures, the desecration of the entire island? How could she participate in the wanton destruction of something so precious and unique? Because it was her job? Because someone paid her?

Bile rose in her throat. Annabel was right. She had lost all perspective. She should have sought professional help years ago.

Annabel had been horrified when Grace told her, clinically

and coldly, what had happened five years ago. She had been raped by a group of men, left for dead, and had been in a coma for almost two months. The police had pieced together the story from the evidence unwittingly provided by her body. Grace still couldn't remember a thing...no faces, no voices, no distinguishing characteristics, nothing. All she had was The Dream, and all memory of that dissipated the moment she woke.

Annabel had urged her to get some therapy when she got back home. Grace had mixed feelings about the idea. She had been telling the truth when she said she felt nothing, no emotion at all. Five years had passed since she woke up in that hospital bed. She enjoyed life. Why dredge up an experience that could only damage her peace of mind? It was not as if she were depressed or sexually dysfunctional. Far from it. She felt perfectly fine and had as many sexual partners as she wanted.

She thought about Dawn, about the surprising comfort of lying in her arms last night when she surfaced, sweating and panicked, from The Dream. Shrugging off a sharp sense of loss, she reminded herself that Dawn was just a kid looking for romance—passionate declarations on moonlit beaches. She would pine after Grace for a few days, then find some other sweet young thing to hold hands with. Puppy love. It was hardly Grace's style.

DAWN'S HEAD SWUM. For a moment she lay very still, staring at the pillow next to hers. The impression of another head bore silent testament to what had transpired in this bed. Blushing, Dawn, stretched gingerly. She felt tender between her legs, another lingering reminder. Her gaze traveled slowly around the room, halting at the window.

Grace was sitting on the verandah, staring out to sea.

Dawn watched her, unseen. It was time to say goodbye, she thought, feeling utterly desolate. It seemed unreal. They had only just met. Surely what had happened between them was too important, too wonderful, to mean nothing. Her womb fluttered in accord.

Dawn swung her legs to the floor. Belting a silk kimono around her waist, she headed unsteadily out of the bedroom. She felt dizzy. Her hands were clammy and a leaden pain in her thighs reminded her that she hadn't taken any medication in almost two days.

In the kitchen, she propped herself against the counter and plunged her hand into the cookie jar. She had to lift her blood sugar, and quickly. Then she would dose up. Doggedly she chewed several tasteless crackers in quick succession. They felt hideously insecure in her stomach. A film of perspiration collected across her forehead. Saliva pooled in her mouth. She was going to be sick, Dawn realized.

She made it to the bathroom only seconds before she threw up. Footsteps rapidly followed.

"Dawn? Are you all right?" Grace wrenched open the door.

"What does it look like?" Dawn turned toward the woman hovering in the doorway. Immediately, she wished she could exchange her response for something sweeter and more winning.

Grace seemed at a loss. "God, you look ill."

It was obvious what she was thinking. What was wrong with Dawn? Did she have some rare tropical disease? Was it fatal? Was it contagious? "It's just the DTs," Dawn explained dryly. "I haven't taken any painkillers in forty-eight hours."

"Are you saying you're addicted?"

Dawn raised her chin. "I'm saying I'm in pain, and I'm having a hard time getting off my medication."

"Are you sure you should be doing that?" Grace scrutinized her. "I mean, there's no crime in pain relief."

"Sure." Dawn rinsed a washcloth and mopped her face. "Only I don't want to spend the rest of my life popping pills, that's all."

Grace looked awkward, her eyes straying to Dawn's legs. "Will you ever—"

"Walk perfectly again?" Dawn finished on a brittle note. "Probably not. Why do you ask?"

"I just wondered." Feeble, Grace thought. She had to go, she reminded herself emphatically. This was not the time to begin a deep and meaningful conversation.

After Dawn brushed her teeth and rinsed her mouth a few times, they moved to the verandah.

"Feeling better now?"

Dawn nodded. "I'm sorry I was so grumpy." Staring at Grace, with unveiled emotion, she begged, "Please don't go."

Grace's mouth dried. Complications. "I don't have any choice. Annabel and Cody aren't real happy about what I've been doing here."

Dawn gave her a strange look. "Cody knows?"

"I'm sure Annabel has told her."

Dawn colored. For a moment it seemed she would say something else, then she sat down, eyes dropping to the painted wooden verandah boards. After a long pause, she said. "Does it bother you that I have a limp?"

Momentarily disoriented by the change of subject, Grace

took a moment to respond. "Not in the way you seem to think. It bothers me because I like you. I want to see you fully recovered."

"Do you?" The response was strained. "Want to see me, that is?" Chin tilted defensively, eyes full of hope, Dawn looked unbearably young.

Grace sagged back into her chair. "Sure I do." She injected her voice with a flippancy she didn't feel. "If you're ever in New York, look me up."

"That's not what I meant."

This conversation needed to stop right here, Grace decided.

"I'm asking if I matter to you." Dawn's blue eyes shone bright with emotion. She looked profoundly vulnerable sitting there naked beneath her kimono, her damaged legs shaking slightly. "I'm asking if last night meant anything?"

Grace cursed inwardly, furious at herself all of a sudden. She should never have come here. She should have written that note. She needed to say goodbye and remember Dawn as two hot nights on a tropical island. Period. No drama. No illusions. Knowing that Dawn had developed feelings for her was a burden.

"I had fun last night." She managed her most offhand morning-after tone. "Maybe we can repeat it sometime."

Dawn paled. "That's it?"

"Look, I have to go." Grace stood.

"You feel nothing? Felt nothing?" Dawn's face radiated disbelief.

Grace shoved her feet into her sandals. "I said I enjoyed it, Dawn." She raised her voice slightly. "Can't we just leave it at that, for God's sake. I don't want to hurt you."

"Then why are you lying to me?"

"I'm not lying!" Her voice reverberated across the still morning air.

Dawn's eyes blazed. "I felt something. I felt it here." She slapped her chest with an angry fist. "And so did you. You're just too chicken to admit it!"

"What!" Grace's hands shook. This was too much. Why the hell had she waited around here to play Ms. Nice Girl? She should have gone home while the kid was still sleeping. Pinned a goodbye note to the door. "You don't know what you're talking about," she informed Dawn coldly. "I'm the first woman you've ever slept with. That hardly makes you an authority."

"I know what I felt!"

"And I'll tell you what I felt," Grace retorted. "It's called hot, turned on. I felt lust. I wanted to fuck you. End of story."

"I know that. I'm not stupid." Dawn advanced unsteadily

toward her and seized a handful of her shirt. Then she was cry-ing. "Grace, please." It came out all broken. "Remember last night, after your nightmare—"

"No!" Grace wrenched herself free of Dawn's grip, then watched with horror as the younger woman staggered back, off balance.

Even as Grace's arm shot out to prevent her, Dawn crashed down the verandah steps with a cry of agony.

"Oh, God. Dawn." Grace plunged after her. On her knees, she cradled the young woman, listening helplessly to her small animal grunts of pain. "Oh, baby. I'm sorry. I'm so sorry."

Scalding blue eyes met hers. "Get my fucking pills," Dawn gasped. "Then get out of here. I never want to see you again."

SEATED ON GRACE Ramsay's verandah, Cody was so engrossed in her paperback that she didn't notice the copper-haired woman approaching.

"Good book?"

Cody lifted her head, shielding her eyes against the sun. Grace was standing in front of her, looking twitchy, her hands hiding in her pockets. Her face seemed strained. Attributing this to the shameful circumstances of her departure, Cody felt a brief, private pleasure. Served her right.

She couldn't pretend to like Grace Ramsay. It was nothing to do with the fact that she was one of Annabel's castoffs. It was her personality. She was so detached, so self-satisfied. And her conduct made TV evangelists look honorable. Cody made a show of looking at her watch. "You're late," she said bluntly. "Are you ready to leave?"

"Sure. I've just been saying my farewells." Grace idly took the book from Cody's knee and with calm deliberation flipped through a few pages. "Tama Janowitz." Meeting Cody's eyes, she observed, "Yuppie porn doesn't seem quite your style, but what do I know?"

Cody snatched the book back. "A guest left it behind." Why did she feel the need to explain herself to this smart-mouthed bitch?

Grace looked her up and down with shameless candor. "Uh huh."

Infuriated to find herself coloring, Cody asked, "Do you need help with your luggage?"

"I think I can handle it," Grace murmured. She emerged some while later, having showered and changed. "Oh, by the way." She held out a pair of sunglasses, her expression that of a cat remembering a puddle of cream. "Annabel left these here the other night."

Forcing nonchalance, Cody took the sunnies and jammed them into her pocket. Annabel had every right to spend time with Grace. She needed to find out about this Argus stuff. Cody trusted her, didn't she? Dragging herself out of her chair, she lifted a couple of the bags and stalked off along the jungle track toward the beach. Grace would be gone soon enough, she reminded herself. All Cody needed to do was resist the temptation to tip her overboard.

As she pushed the dinghy into the water, she saw Grace turn and stare back at the beach. Up near the palms there was a flash of pink. Cody waved an oar. "Dawn!" she called, then caught an odd glimmer in Grace's eyes.

The woman looked like she'd just murdered someone's puppy. In the grip of growing suspicion, Cody reviewed the events of the morning.

When she'd gone to Grace's cottage, she'd called out and glanced in the windows that faced onto the verandah. Grace's bed was empty and neatly made.

When Grace returned she had taken a shower and changed her clothes, surely the kind of thing you did *before* you went to calling on your neighbor. That is, unless you'd spent the night with her.

Cody eyed Grace. "Have you been sleeping with Dawn?" she demanded accusingly.

Grace's eyes widened. "What's this? Confession?"

"I should have guessed." Cody groaned out loud. "I suppose you just couldn't resist trying your luck."

"And what if I did? What's it to you?"

"Dawn's straight," Cody said sharply.

"Wise up, sweetheart!" Grace gave a brittle laugh. "She might be a homophobe, but she's definitely not straight."

Grace was speaking firsthand. Appalled, Cody thought about Dawn, unhappy and confused, asking questions about lesbians. "You took advantage of her!" she said angrily.

"Someone had to."

The woman was completely degenerate. And she sure as hell rated herself high. "Oh, I get it," Cody said. "You did her a favor."

Grace gave a small expressive whistle. "If I didn't know better, I'd think you were jealous. Come to think of it, Annabel mentioned Dawn has the hots for you." She raised an eyebrow. "Why don't you check her out? I've done all the hard work for you."

Cody blinked in disbelief. She could not be hearing this. Were there no limits to Grace Ramsay's moral delinquency? "Grace," she said in a tone of patient irony. "The next time you open your mouth to make a comment like that, you'll be swallowing ocean."

Grace merely grinned. "I can see why you made such a big impression on Annabel."

Cody gave her a stony look. "I can see why you didn't."

# Chapter
# Fifteen

CHIN CRADLED DESPONDENTLY in her hands, Dawn blew sand off the pages of her Jackie Collins. It was almost an hour since she'd watched Cody and Grace skim away across the glistening water. She hadn't cried, and she wasn't going to. Grace Ramsay wasn't worth it.

Face it, Dawn, she told herself unkindly, you asked for it. You could have kept your pride and said goodbye as if it didn't matter. You could have made no emotional demands. Instead she had taken a risk, hoping the Grace she'd discovered during the night might have lingered. Now she was beginning to think she had imagined her.

Closing her book, she stared broodingly at the empty horizon. She felt drained, years older. So much had happened in so little time. How could she have been blind to something so completely central to who she was? She must have been living in some kind of bubble, imagining the only future she had, apart from swimming, was marriage and children.

Dawn recalled her last Moon Island holiday and cringed. She had been so obnoxious...to Cody in particular. Heat seeped into her cheeks. She'd had a crush on Cody back then, she recognized miserably. It had probably been obvious to everyone but her. She must have made a complete fool of herself.

A thrumming whine caught her attention and she looked up to see a small silver plane climbing away from the island. Annabel and Grace. Her heart turned over. Were they really having an affair? In the end she'd been too chicken to confront Grace. And too busy getting her into bed, she reminded herself with abject shame.

Straining to catch the final fading note of the engine, she felt desperately alone all of a sudden. Grace's cottage was empty and she would never see her again. Leaning heavily on her stick, she started along the track to Frangipani Cottage. Maybe she should just go back home to Sydney. There really wasn't any reason to stay. She'd gone quite far enough for one journey of self-discovery.

She reached the cottage, wandered inside, capsized onto her bed, then lurched straight up again, tears of dismay flooding her eyes. She could smell cloves. With a wrenching sob, she abandoned the bed, tearing the sheets from the mattress and throwing them out the door. She stared around. The very walls seemed to have trapped the echo of Grace's voice, her sighs, her sensual laughter. Dawn's skin prickled with the memory of her touch. Her mouth watered. She could almost taste Grace. With shocking clarity, she felt a sensation deep inside, as if Grace's fingers were still compressed there.

She stared at herself in the mirror and recoiled from the sight of her ripeness. Her body was rounder, her skin pink and glowing. Knowing eyes confronted her, a full expectant mouth. She was aching and moist between her legs, yearning to make love again.

Dawn stumbled out of the room. She couldn't stay here, she thought wildly. It was unbearable. Clumsily she rummaged in the laundry for clean clothes, pulling on loose cotton shorts and a T-shirt. Stuffing a sweater and water flask into her small backpack, she grabbed her Reeboks and headed for the bathroom.

Villa Luna was about three and a half hours' walk. Dawn was certain she could remember the way from riding it the other day with Cody. She fastened her sneakers, checked her pack for the compass and pocket knife, opened the bathroom cupboard and removed her painkillers and the little first aid kit. She wasn't planning on an accident, but it couldn't do any harm to take precautions.

Before she left, she cranked the old-fashioned telephone for Villa Luna and waited, experimentally flexing her legs. There was no pain. The double dose earlier had taken care of that. No one answered the phone and for a moment Dawn deliberated whether to wait and try again. There didn't seem much point. Cody wouldn't mind if she just turned up. And even if she wasn't home, Dawn could let herself in and wait. Guests were allowed to do that.

"YOU CAN REALLY fly this thing," Grace commented as they taxied to a halt in Avarua.

Annabel didn't bother to respond. The startled tone people used when they commented on her flying invariably niggled her. She expected such blatant sexism from men, but it was disappointing that a woman of Grace's intelligence didn't know better.

Annabel helped carry her luggage into the airport lounge. "I'm sorry I can't hang around," she said, "I need to run some errands."

Grace's charcoal eyes drew hers. "So, it's goodbye then."

"I don't expect we'll see one another again." Annabel hesitated. "You will think about what I suggested, won't you?"

"I am thinking about it," Grace said quietly. "Look, I—"

"It's okay," Annabel had no plans to revisit the subject of Argus Chemco. Grace had made her choices. Annabel was not going to judge her. "Really."

Grace looked uncharacteristically awkward. "Will you do me a favor?" She scrawled something on a piece of paper and folded it across the middle. "Could you give this to Dawn, please?"

Annabel tucked the note into her jacket. She knew Grace well enough to know it could only mean one thing. "Don't tell me you've been messing with youthful emotions."

Grace responded with a shadowed version of her lopsided grin. "She's very cute."

Envisioning the scenario, Annabel rolled her eyes. "Pick on someone your own size next time."

"It's not like she didn't want it," Grace was predictably defensive. "But if I'd known she was so..."

"So vulnerable? Are you telling me you didn't notice? Please."

"She'll get over it," Grace said. "I just can't handle the emotional stuff. Maybe I've got a hang-up or something."

"Remarkable observation."

"I didn't mean to hurt her."

Annabel compressed her lips. "Grace," she said mildly. "They're going to put that on your tombstone." She leaned forward, kissed her one-time lover lightly on the mouth and murmured goodbye.

"Don't forget the note," Grace called after her.


THREE HOURS LATER Annabel stuck her head into the hangar. "Smithy?"

The place was dead quiet, no sign of the elderly mechanic. Puzzled, Annabel strolled across the tarmac to the Dominie. The plane had obviously been serviced. Smithy had turned it around ready for take-off, and the cargo was fully loaded. He usually waited until she was airborne before he packed up for the day.

Just as Annabel was clambering aboard, she spotted a wiry figure waving as he approached. "Lucky I caught yer." Smithy thrust a small parcel at her. "Emergency drop," he explained with his customary economy of communication. "Mitiaro."

Annabel examined the parcel with a sinking heart. It bore a Red Cross seal and was flagged urgent. "This is going to take hours," she groaned.

The mechanic eyed her sympathetically. "Just missed the tourist charter," he rasped. "Some darn fool forgot to give it to 'em."

Annabel dropped the parcel onto the seat. She couldn't refuse to take it. Bevan operated an informal emergency shuttle around the islands, dropping medical supplies and performing the occasional porcine cesarean. She supposed she should be grateful she'd been spared the latter.

"Well, I'd better give her some stick," she grumbled, belting herself in. The trip would take four hours out of her schedule and if anything went wrong refueling on Mitiaro, she'd be stuck there overnight. Wonderful. The island was only slightly more famous for its eels than the swamps they lived in. As for accommodation, she'd probably have to sleep on the plane.

Smithy reached inside his overalls. "I've logged yer flight plan." He handed Annabel a dog-eared copy. "The old trooper's runnin' like a dream." He ran his gnarled fingers affectionately across the Dominie's undercarriage.

Annabel clipped the flight plan to her board. "You know, right now a Lear sounds like a really good idea."

Smithy gazed at her as if she'd taken leave of her senses. "For them as can't fly a real plane, maybe."

# Chapter
# Seventeen

DAWN STARED UP at the sun and hoisted her T-shirt out of her shorts. Sweat beaded her face. She'd been walking for two hours and had finally crossed the northwestern ridge.

Checking her compass and her watch, she smiled at her own progress. Who said Dawn Beaumont was a write-off? She remembered the last time she had crossed the *makatea*. She had been with two other women and they were returning to Villa Luna after sheltering from the hurricane. One of the women was injured, and they'd had to carry her part of the way.

They'd gotten hopelessly lost after some fool dropped the compass, and Dawn had wondered if they would ever make it. Back then it had seemed impossible. Now, she was amazed she could have been so frightened. Moon Island was a tiny place. You could walk from one side to the other in a day. Even if you did get lost, you only had to head for the ocean and take the long route around the island.

The only real danger was the *makatea*. Although it was overgrown with jungle, the fossilized coral reef was still razor sharp. But so long as you watched your step you couldn't really go wrong.

Picking her way through the dense jungle in the center of the island, Dawn paced herself to avoid getting heat exhaustion. By her calculations, Villa Luna was about an hour and a half away. Guessing she must be somewhere near the cave they had sheltered in during the hurricane, she examined her surroundings with a surge of excitement. The jungle had a frightening uniformity about it. Thank God for compasses and pocketknives.

Dawn carved a notch into the palm she'd been leaning against and mopped her face with the hem of her t-shirt. Glancing at her watch once more, she wondered idly if she could find the Kopeka cave. There was plenty of time and the idea was oddly tempting. She decided she'd give it half an hour. If she didn't locate the cave by then, she would simply carry on to Villa Luna.

BLEARY-EYED, CODY plucked her paperback off her chest and crossed the sitting room to gaze out the window. Annabel wouldn't be back for hours. Instead of lying about indoors like a couch potato, she ought to find something to do. It was too hot to work on any of her building projects. Maybe she could go fishing or just hoon around in the boat. The new Mercury outboard was really something. Two hundred horsepower. Time to dust off the water skis.

Wondering if Dawn was home, Cody tried the phone. No answer. Doubtless the young Australian was consoling herself with Jackie Collins and junk food. Cody had a feeling Dawn might appreciate some company. God knows, she could probably use a shoulder to cry on having just come off second-best with Grace Ramsay. Gathering up her fishing gear and her bathing suit, she wrote a note to Annabel and headed for the beach.

The runabout was hot from the afternoon sun. Chugging out of Passion Bay, Cody turned her face thankfully to the breeze. Sometimes the heat of the tropics got to her. After Wellington, New Zealand, with its long winters and bitter southerly gales, Moon Island felt like a permanent hothouse. Every now and then Cody found herself yearning for a cold, miserable day just for old times' sake.

She anchored off Hibiscus Bay, changed into her sedate swimsuit, and swam ashore. One day soon they were going to build a jetty here. They'd had the plans drawn up recently. With decent facilities, they would be able to land enough materials to build several new cottages on this part of the island.

Cody wasn't crazy about extending their operations, but these days they were always booked out, which made it almost impossible to get away from the island for a break. Annabel thought that adding extra accommodations would take some pressure off their bookings and make it easier to create regular space in their calendar. It would be a pleasant change to be all alone on the island with her lover once in a while, Cody thought.

The beach was deserted, no sign of Dawn. Calling her name, Cody strolled into the jungle and up the slope to Frangipani Cottage. She knocked on the front door, walked around the building, then flopped down on a cane chair on the verandah. Dawn must have taken a walk, she concluded. On the other hand, why would Dawn, who needed help to make it more than fifty paces, go for a walk in the jungle without telling anyone?

There was no note on the door, and Dawn hadn't phoned in a plan for the hiking log. A guest on the island twice, she was well aware of the rules. A crawling uneasiness overtook Cody and she stared at the silent cottage, full of misgivings. What if it had all been too much for Dawn—the accident, her ruined career, seduction by the sleazy Grace? Could she have done Something Stupid?

Cody's imagination generated a bloody suicide in a bath, a comatose Dawn clutching an empty sleeping-pill bottle. Lurching to her feet, she pushed open the unlocked front door and barged into the cottage, shouting Dawn's name.

The sitting room was empty, a Jackie Collins novel face down on the coffee table. Evidence of a meal littered the kitchen counter. Cody stumbled over a pile of sheets in front of the bedroom door and stared into the room. Nothing. Just the faintest hint of a spicy scent lingering in the air.

Frowning, she scoured the cottage, this time concentrating on detail. She pulled open the bathroom cabinet, slammed the mirrored door, then paused and opened it again. Where was the first aid kit? And Dawn's pills? Cody could recall seeing several large bottles of painkillers last time she was here helping Mrs. Marsters with the housekeeping.

After checking the kitchen for the pills, she searched the bedroom without success. Why would Dawn take those bottles with her instead of one or two tablets? Tripping over a pair of sandals near the closet, Cody caught a sharp image of the younger woman tying her Reeboks the day she came out fishing. Where were those sneakers?

Cody rummaged in the bedroom closet, marched through the cottage, and gazed around the verandah. Finally, in puzzled silence, she sat down in the cane chair once more and considered the clues. Dawn wasn't home. She was wearing her Reeboks. She had taken the first aid kit and all her painkillers. There was only one conclusion to be drawn. Dawn had decided to go deep into the jungle, take all those pills, lie down under a palm tree, and end it all.

Latching firmly onto the negative fantasy, Cody ran back indoors and filled her water flask. She had to find Dawn before it was too late!

It occurred to her that there was one big hole in her theory. The note. A grief-stricken twenty-two year old would leave a note. She might even write several attempts. Trying to think like a detective, Cody lifted the lid off the trash and rifled through. Heart pounding, she plucked a balled sheet of paper from a mound of banana skins, and, smoothing it out, read:

*Dear Cody,*

*There's something I need to tell you, but I feel really bad about it. I was passing Grace's cottage a couple of nights ago and I saw her and Annabel. They were making out on the verandah. I'm really sorry.*

*You probably won't believe this. Why would you, since I've been so horrible to you and Annabel? But it's the truth.*

*I know I've never been a friend to you, but you've been one to me and I'm grateful for that. So this letter is my way of being a friend to you, because if you can't trust your friends to tell you if something is going on, who can you trust?*

*Yours sincerely,*
*Dawn Beaumont*

Stunned, Cody sank down in the nearest chair and stared at the letter. Annabel and Grace. It didn't make any sense. Yet... She thought about Annabel defending the woman, her obvious unease around Grace at the airstrip a few hours ago. Cody had put it down to disgust and embarrassment over Grace's role in the Argus drama. But maybe something else was going on.

Anger, hot and mindless, boiled in her veins. She wanted to kill Grace Ramsay! Slinging her flask over her shoulder, she stormed out of the cottage. She had to find Dawn. If the letter had been written to make trouble, she would wring that girl's neck. But, if it was the truth? Cody felt sick at heart.


SIMMERING WITH FRUSTRATION, Grace checked into the Rarotongan Resort Hotel. It was just her luck—stuck for three days before she could get a plane out of here! All this and the deal was off anyway. By now, Hausmann must have ceased licking his wounds and would doubtless be cultivating some military dictator looking to trade land for firepower. Grace couldn't see why Argus didn't expand its dumping operations in China or Mexico. But Hausmann was hellbent on a Pacific presence. It would make Argus so very attractive to the Japanese, clients and investors alike.

Grace wondered gloomily how many more islands she would have to assess, how many reports she would write, sealing the doom of thousands of living creatures, entire eco-systems. Where would it end? What kind of world would it be when there were no pristine islands left to destroy, no more rainforests to convert to cheap packaging, no polar ice caps, no way to turn back the climatic clock?

Her own role in the systematic ecocide of the planet was insignificant, yet did that free her of culpability? When was 'following orders' an acceptable excuse for participating in acts that were not only unethical, but morally criminal? Would generations one day look back, as she did at Nazi Germany, and wonder how a group of greedy, amoral bullies in the late twentieth century could have hijacked an entire people and imposed an agenda so insane no one could believe it even as it was happening beneath their noses?

She thought about Robert Hausmann's standard response to the various environmentalists who opposed Argus initiatives. *The future is not my problem.* Maybe he had a point. Was it mere self-indulgence to get squeamish all of a sudden about earning a living doing what she did? How exactly would it help save the planet if Grace Ramsay walked away from the career she had invested ten years to build?

Jaded, she phoned New York.

Camille Marquez took the call. Hausmann, she explained, was in Tokyo finalizing the first big dumping contract for Moon Island.

"What?" Grace was taken aback. "I understood the deal went cold."

There was a pause. "I think you should talk with Mr. Hausmann about that."

"Are you saying the owner has agreed to sell?" Grace's head spun. There was no way Annabel would have made an about-face. She felt certain of that. Camille must have misunderstood.

"I'm saying as far as I know the project is proceeding as planned," Camille replied coolly.

"Well." Grace forced neutrality into her tone. "Evidently there's some information I don't have." After supplying Camille with her arrival details, she hung up.

In the few hours since they arrived in Rarotonga, Annabel couldn't possibly have changed her mind. And if she had... Grace warded off images of the island leveled, warning signs everywhere, the reef filled with suppurating waste. Anxiously twisting her earring, she called a taxi and strode from her room.


ANNABEL HAD FLOWN to Mitiaro a few times on mercy dashes with Bevan. The island was the smallest of the volcanic group lying northeast of Rarotonga. Tourists didn't bother with it much. It was flat and mostly swamp, crawling with biting insects, and there was nothing to eat except eels and bananas. A couple of hundred islanders subsisted there. Every now and then, someone had an accident and the local dispensary called Rarotonga for supplies. It was a good excuse to gossip on the wireless, and entice a pilot to airlift additional goodies from Avarua.

After a couple of hours, Annabel started watching for the familiar dotting of islands that signaled her destination. Theoretically she should be right over Atiu, with Bevan's and Don's place a mere pineapple's toss away. She peered out at the turquoise ocean, removed her aviators, squinted around, then put them back on and studied her instruments.

She was bearing northeast at two thousand feet, dead on course. Yet there was no island in sight. She tapped her compass lightly. The reading was unchanged. Shrugging she radioed Mitiaro. A cloud of static hissed back at her. She checked her frequency and the radio whined in protest. Niggled, she examined her flight plan.

Everything seemed straightforward. She was on course, on time, and supposedly just minutes away from landing on Mitiaro's moth-eaten airstrip. Annabel glanced at her fuel gauge, then stared, riveted. Full. It read full. Impossible. She tapped the dial sharply. The needle appeared to be stuck.

"Fuck," she cursed. "Damn and shit."

Her immediate impulse was to drop airspeed and conserve fuel, but she made a conscious effort to control her leaping pulse and collect her wits. Making decisions out of panic was not the way to handle this situation. The horizon spread before her, barren shimmering blue, and suddenly Annabel thought that flying over an empty ocean must be the loneliest feeling on earth. Amelia Earhart had done it, and Jean Batten and hundreds of other aviators, some of them in craft that made the Dominie look as sophisticated as a B-2 Stealth Bomber.

Mitiaro was one of a group of islands. Assuming she was no more than a few degrees off course one way or the other, she should still be able to sight them. Annabel gazed ahead, willing a land mass to rise from the sleeping ocean.

There was probably some simple explanation, she reasoned, a silly error on the flight plan. If she could just locate it and work her way backward, calculate her position. She still had fuel, even if her gauge had malfunctioned. The Dominie's range was nearly five hundred miles. She had enough fuel to get back to Rarotonga—provided she turned back now, that was. And to do that, she needed some accurate bearings.

Frowning, she banked right, half circled, banked left. There was nothing in sight, just ocean. She looked hard at her compass and her mouth went dry. If her compass was to be believed, the sun was in the wrong place. Instrument failure? Rare and unusual for a DH Dominie. Originally built as air force naviga- tion trainers, the old biplanes had, for their time, the most advanced and reliable instruments available.

Annabel rapidly performed some mental gymnastics. She had around a hundred minutes of fuel left and had completely lost her bearings. If she climbed a little and worked with the slight tailwind she could drop her airspeed from the usual 105 mph back to around 90 and maybe stretch her air time to two hours. Surely she could locate at least one of the Cook Islands in that time frame.

Tuning into the International Distress Frequency, she put out a CQ. There was no reply. Commercial aircraft were sup- posed to stay tuned into this frequency, but obviously there were none in the area. Cursing the lack of a long range HF radio, she tried again, only this time registered an SOS. Then she just flew.

As time crept by, Annabel found herself listening with pain- ful concentration for the telltale splutter of an engine failing. You're going to die, she thought numbly. How could this have happened? It was too unfair. Cody's face materialized before her, gray eyes appealing. "Do you have to fly so much? I worry about you terribly."

Annabel was stricken. What if this really was the end? What if she never saw Cody again, never held her. There would be no goodbyes, no chance to tell her how much she loved her. A dry sob wrenched at her throat and she found herself bargaining with God. *Please don't let me die, I'll do anything.*

Wet with adrenalin induced sweat, she studied her wrist- watch. She had fifteen minutes of fuel left. Maybe less. The bar- ren ocean taunted her anew and she logged yet another mayday, desperately conscious of being unable to state her position. Her omni was depressingly silent, not entirely surprising given the nearest VOR station was probably out of range.

She wondered if anyone had picked up the mayday signals she had been transmitting continuously. If, by some miracle, she could ditch her plane into the ocean and survive, would she be found? The Pacific was a vast search area. Knowing she was fly- ing to Mitiaro, Search & Rescue would concentrate on that route. They would be looking in the wrong place.

Annabel groped beneath her seat, found a dusty life jacket and slipped it over her head. With icy detachment, she replayed everything Bevan Mitchell had ever taught her about crash land- ings. On the water—glide in, belly flop, bail out immediately or head up the tail and hack your way out. All of the Dominie's weight was up front. She would hit the water, float for a few seconds, then nosedive.

Annabel felt inside her clothing, located her Swiss Army knife, and congratulated herself on being prepared for anything. She could open a can, kill a fish, reflect the sun off an open blade to attract the attention of a rescue craft. In short, survival was child's play. She laughed, a harsh hollow sound.

Fixing her gaze dully on the horizon, she imagined herself in Cody's arms, felt her warmth so vividly that a curious calm settled on her. She thought of Boston, her parents, Aunt Annie. She thought about her lonely childhood, the meaningless existence until, by some miracle, everything changed and there was Moon Island and Cody. Oh my love, she thought bitterly. How could fate be so cruel?

There was a spluttering cough, and she gazed wildly at her starboard engine. She was running out of fuel. In a few minutes the Dominie would start losing altitude. They would glide for a while, unlike a modern aircraft, then drop lower and lower until they plunged into the ocean.

Annabel lowered her nose to maintain airspeed at the expense of altitude and began a gradual descent. They said drowning was a painless way to go. She stared dubiously at the ocean, blinked and rubbed her eyes. Disbelief vied with elation. Directly ahead of her a gray-green blemish encroached on the endless blue. A mirage? She dropped a little more altitude, tried to ignore the hiccup of a propeller, reached for her binoculars.

A tiny atoll lay some five or six tantalizing minutes ahead of her. As she drew closer, Annabel could make out the pink circle of a reef, a milky blue lagoon, white sand, clusters of palm trees. She could almost hear Bevan. Have you ever flown a glider, kid? That's what you've got when you've got no power.

Dropping more height, she eased back the throttle, tossing up between ditching the Dominie in the lagoon or plowing into the beach. On the face of it, the lagoon seemed the obvious choice, but Annabel had never been much of a swimmer and somehow dry land seemed more of a known quantity. She assessed the thin white belt of sand. Landing on such a soft surface, a somersault was almost unavoidable and probably fatal.

To make a successful crash landing she needed to keep her nose up, but not so far up that she landed on her tail. Or she had to risk a deliberate belly flop, smashing her undercarriage so the Dominie would just grind to a halt. Banking left a few degrees, she straightened for an approach. The belt of wet sand parallel to the water's edge would be a firmer, smoother surface than the dry sand higher on the beach.

She almost laughed as her port engine spluttered and died.

Cutting both engines, Annabel focused on keeping aligned with her target, and moments later, the Dominie swanned into the waterline, absorbing the impact with a sickening crunch. Undercarriage crumpling like paper, the little silver plane plowed violently along the beach, one wing skimming the tide, the other closing fast on a stand of coconut palms.

The clearance simply wasn't there. Collecting a tree trunk with one wing, the Dominie spun about face, and with a hideous tearing sound, the fuselage ripped apart. When finally the biplane came to rest, its tail had separated completely and the nose was buried in sand. Inside the cockpit Annabel smiled once, then slumped over the column, blood pooling around her feet.

# Chapter
# Eighteen

GRACE STUMBLED THROUGH the hangar doorway and yelled, "Hello! Is anybody there?"

From the opposite wall a small, grizzled-looking man in a white overall peered over his shoulder. "Lookin' fer someone, miss?"

"You're from London!" Grace exclaimed, moving inside.

"John Smith at yer service," he rasped. "You obviously 'aven't been living at 'ome fer a fair while."

"No, I live in New York these days. I'm Grace Ramsay."

The old man eyed her sharply. "Wotcha doin' in that 'ell-hole?"

Grace grinned. "Leading a life of moral depravity, Mr. Smith."

"They call me Smithy round 'ere." A pair of bright sparrow-eyes sized her up. "You lookin' for 'erself?"

"Annabel? Yes. I need to see her urgently."

"Too late." He shook his head. "Flew out a few hours back. But the guvnor's due any time. Need a ride, I daresay 'e'll oblige."

The governor? Annabel had mentioned a pilot she employed. "No. I don't need a ride," she said. "I'm staying here on Rarotonga."

"Yer weren't out 'ere lookin' for 'er before?"

Grace shook her head. Before?

"Jes' wonderin'. Found these." Smithy reached into a pocket and produced a pair of pliers.

Grace turned them over in her hand. "Not mine."

The weathered old man pocketed them indifferently. "Finders keepers."

Losers weepers. Grace thought again about Robert Hausmann. She still couldn't believe Annabel had changed her mind about selling. "Smithy," she said. "Can we contact Annabel on Moon Island?"

He scratched his head. "Won't be there yet. She'll be on Mitiaro, I reckon."

"Mitiaro?"

"Northern Group...'mergency medical drop. We could radio."

Grace brightened. Annabel would probably laugh at her. No doubt Camille had it all wrong. Besides, what was she planning to say if Annabel had decided to sell? Make some groveling plea for conservation? What a joke coming from her.

Daunted, she listened as Smithy radioed Mitiaro and conducted a conversation in some strange vernacular. His expression underwent a curious shift, and his watery blue eyes widened. Something in his face made her mouth go dry.

"What is it?" she demanded as soon as he'd signed off.

"She's not there," Smithy said stiffly and immediately lit a cigarette. His hands shook. "She never made it."


DAWN EASED HERSELF into the mouth of the Kopeka Cave, blinking rapidly to accustom herself to the dimness. The cave was not completely dark. Daylight shafted into the limestone chambers through a series of narrow chimneys which also provided conduits for the thousands of Kopeka birds that made their home in the cave. There was a flurry of wings as Dawn padded into the fusty interior, and the tiny swallows swooped low, strafing her like bats. Waving her arms, she shooed them off. Somehow they didn't bother her the way they had the first time she was here.

Dawn felt a strange nostalgia when she reached the hollow where they had sat out the hurricane. Nudging the charred residue of a fire with her toe, she remembered that night with a pang. What a horrible brat she'd been back then, constantly complaining and making thoughtless remarks to her companions.

At the time, she had not appreciated what the experience would really mean to her. Having survived the whole ordeal, she had returned to Sydney with a new sense of her own power. That confidence had paid off in her swimming, giving her the tiny edge that made the difference in the final few yards of a race.

Dawn knew her experiences on Moon Island had also helped her survive her accident. She had tried to get Lynda out of the mangled passenger seat. Then, realizing her teammate was dead, she had somehow dragged herself from the wreckage of the car. Had she stayed where she was, waiting to be rescued, she would have burned to death. If there was anything the hurricane and its aftermath had taught her, it was that she had no idea what she was really capable of until she had to do it.

Sitting opposite the long dead embers, Dawn smiled to herself, realizing she had been dragged, kicking and screaming, into adulthood on this island. The process had begun with Hurricane Mary and ended with an emotional earthquake named Grace Ramsay. Dawn hardly knew what to think or feel any more. She was distressed over what had transpired with Grace, yet on another level she felt oddly empowered. Her identity lay not in what she could achieve, but in who she really was. And, finally, she was getting to know herself.

Dawn gazed up at the limestone ceiling. She had never noticed how pretty it was, how the caves amplified sound. She called out her name and listened as it resonated through the connecting caverns. Giggling at this childish impulse, she took a long drink from her water flask. Her stomach rumbled as the cool liquid settled. She was hungry, starving in fact. She'd felt so sick when she fled the cottage that it hadn't occurred to her to bring any food.

Mouth watering, Dawn recalled the bananas she'd seen drooping from the palms around the cave. They couldn't be that hard to reach. She scrambled to her feet and returned to the brilliance of the afternoon. There was a palm only a few yards away. Attention fastened greedily on an enormous bunch of stubby pinkish bananas, she clutched at the fleshy protrusions that laddered the thick trunk and grappled her way toward the fruit.

The bananas fell with satisfying thuds into the foliage below. When she had accounted for at least twenty or so, Dawn slithered down to the ground and set about retrieving them. Sitting happily beside her cache, she gobbled one pink banana after the next. They were not quite ripe, but she didn't care. Smaller and sweeter than the yellow kind you got in the supermarket, they were called Ladyfingers.

Dawn found herself blushing over the expression and the wayward train of thought it provoked. Gathering up the remaining few bananas, she stuffed them into her pack for the hike to Villa Luna.

Barely had she walked for five minutes, when the first violent pains struck. Panting, Dawn collapsed against a papaya, her mind instantly flooded with garbled imaginings about food poisoning and tropical diseases. The pain was excruciating, stabbing her directly below her ribs where twelve poorly chewed bananas had descended on her empty pill-damaged stomach. A classic case of banana belly.

Groaning, Dawn curled into a ball. Tears of frustration rolled down her cheeks. Why couldn't anything go right for her?

What had she ever done that was so terrible she had to pay for it with wrecking her legs, turning into some kind of sexual weirdo, and now dying of banana poisoning in the middle of nowhere?

Her father would say the Lord moves in mysterious ways.

"Bastard!" Dawn yelled at the heavens.

# Chapter
# Nineteen

THE LATE AFTERNOON sun lolled low in the sky. Dawn's letter in her pocket, Cody trudged through the jungle, worried and angry at the same time. Before setting off across the *makatea*, she had stopped by Grace's cottage just in case Dawn had decided to return to the scene of the crime, as it were.

But the more Cody thought about it, the more obvious it seemed. Depressed, Dawn had plunged aimlessly into the jungle. By now, she could be anywhere on the island. Cody tried not to picture her bleeding to death at the bottom of some gully, having cut herself to ribbons on the *makatea*. One person, searching on foot, would have almost no chance of finding her.

She stared helplessly around. Dawn might be hysterical, but she was still walking with a stick. Logically that meant she must have taken the easiest trail. Heartened, Cody headed north for Villa Luna.

When she found the first piece of white rag tied to a papaya leaf, she thought little of it. Guests often marked a meeting spot this way, and Cody made a point of removing such markers as she found them to keep the environment pristine. She must have missed this one. But a hundred yards further along the trail, there was a newly carved notch in a tree trunk, then another white rag hanging from a branch.

Despite herself, Cody was impressed. The Dawn of three years ago would never have considered such practicalities, and surely no one bent on a quiet suicide somewhere in the jungle would bother to leave a trail. Relief flooded her as she followed the freshly trampled vegetation. Her quarry appeared to be heading toward the center of the island. It all made sense now. Needing a shoulder to cry on, Dawn had decided to walk to Villa Luna. Perhaps she was already there.

Cody stopped in her tracks. It would be silly to keep on walking if Dawn was twiddling her thumbs at Villa Luna. Annabel was due back soon, and Cody needed to talk to Dawn first.

Quickening her pace, she turned back and headed for the beach.

In the runabout, it took less than ten minutes to reach Villa Luna. Dawn wasn't there and neither was Annabel. Pacing the verandah, Cody glumly examined the sky. She tried not to draw the paranoid conclusion that Annabel had decided to spend a night or two on Rarotonga with Grace and would invent some plausible excuse when she got home. Plane repairs, naturally. It would not be the first time. Bits were always falling off that damned Dominie.

Thank God Bevan would be back soon. They'd had a message that he'd bought another plane. Cody could picture it already—grunty motors, a flashy high-tech instrument panel, and comfortable seats. Finally they would be able to put that old hack out to pasture. Then at least if Annabel had to fly something, it would be modern and well-equipped. For about the thousandth time, Cody wished Annabel would hang up her aviators and get a real hobby. Something safe. What was wrong with knitting?

Reclining on the chaise lounge at the far end of the verandah, Cody drifted off for a while then woke with a start, inhaling the twilight smell of the jungle. Annabel wouldn't be coming home now. She never flew this late. Cody pictured her sitting in the Banana Court with Grace, laughing...their hands idly touching. The thought made her crazy. She couldn't believe it. Annabel would never do that to her, to them.

Cody wiped away the tears that threatened to spill. Where the hell was Dawn? There was barely enough light to saddle up Kahlo and start looking for her. If she'd gotten lost en route to Villa Luna, she'd just have to spend the night in the jungle and let that be a lesson to her.

Cody heaved a loud sigh. Why couldn't other people be more straightforward? Cody didn't have dangerous hobbies. She didn't limp off with a walking stick on some jungle trek because she was having a bad day. Sometimes she felt like the only normal person on the planet in town.

Stuffing an extra pillow behind her head, she took her paperback off the nearby table and contemplated its jacket for a moment. Yuppie porn! That bitch should talk. Grace bloody Ramsay, she thought grimly. This entire fiasco was her doing.


AS DUSK ENVELOPED Avarua, Grace followed Smithy back to the hangar. "I just can't believe this!" she exploded. "An oil tanker reports a possible SOS three hundred miles out of here and nobody does a thing. What sort of outfit is this?"

The head of Air Traffic Control had just informed them that since there were no flight plans active for that area, they had asked a Silk & Boyd freighter to respond. Ms. Worth was bound for Mitiaro, he pointed out, nowhere near the location of the distress signal, which was, by the way, an expanse of empty sea.

He had indicated the general area on a map and said they weren't planning a search at this stage because Annabel must have put down on one of the other islands for some reason. "Something was obviously called in," he said, indicating the flight plan. "I'm sure we'll know more tomorrow."

"I don't get it." Grace tossed her hat down on a chair and paced around the hangar. "She was supposed to have landed on Mitiaro hours ago but hasn't. They have no idea where she is. They can't raise her on the radio. What the fuck are they waiting for?"

Smithy wiped a gnarled hand across his thin gray hair. "Thing I can't fathom is how them bleedin' plans got filed in the first place."

"What do you mean?"

"They was stamped," the mechanic rasped. "Arrival confirmed."

Grace finally understood the significance of that. "You don't think anything was called in?" she asked. "You're saying someone could have filed them showing that she had arrived when she hadn't?"

Smithy nodded. "Stamped her plan by mistake, I s'pose. When some other guy called in. Bloody careless."

"So when the SOS came in they thought she had already landed, so they didn't make the connection," Grace mused aloud. "Oh, my God," she whispered. "She's crashed."

The little mechanic seemed smaller than ever. He was crying, Grace realized. "Better radio Moon Island," he finally mumbled. "Could be she changed 'er plans and headed straight back there."

Grace froze. What would they say to Cody if Annabel wasn't there? That they had no idea where she was? She felt physically sick at the prospect. You couldn't just radio someone and tell her the woman she loved had probably crashed her plane. Her mind wandered to Annabel. Dead? Was it possible?

Shaken, she faced Smithy. "We can't do that. We need to go out there."

Smithy was preoccupied. "Listen." He raised a silencing hand and walked outside, head cocked.

Grace traipsed after him. She couldn't hear a thing. Just the occasional birdcall, car motors firing, the sound of voices somewhere, a child crying.

"It's the guvnor," Smithy announced after another minute of silence.

Grace surveyed the graying sky without optimism. "I can't see anything."

"Nor'east." Smithy pointed.

Either he had X-ray vision or he was going senile. "I could go and see about chartering a plane," Grace volunteered.

"Won't be needin' that, Miss."

"We can't just stand around here and do nothing!" Stuffing her hands into her pockets, Grace prepared to argue the case for another plane when she saw it too; the faintest speck. Riveted, she focused her attention on the tiny black spot. A faint hum grew louder. Relief surged through her limbs.

Smithy extracted a packet of cigarettes from his top pocket and offered her one. Grace took it. They watched the speck draw nearer and nearer. Smithy suddenly let out a long whistle, stubbed out his cigarette, and rushed off into the hangar. He returned moments later with a pair of chocks and a huge tobacco-stained grin. "The lad went and done it," he said as they watched the plane descend. "Ain't she a beauty?"

# Chapter
# Twenty

VIOLET HAZEL WAS talking to herself. Although it was a habit to which she had resigned herself, she had never entirely accepted it. At the age of seventy, the specter of senility loomed all too large. What could once be put down to eccentricity suddenly assumed more sinister connotations.

"I believe you're Lucy Adams." Violet addressed the pale-haired woman lying unconscious in her spare bed. She could remember the child so well, a fairylike creature with white hair and the most astonishing lavender eyes.

Violet had been living on Rarotonga, working as a nurse. That was how she had come to meet the two women who lived on Moon Island, Rebecca and Annie. They used to bring the child in for checkups as often as they could catch the steamer. What a pair they were. Dark-haired Rebecca, dressed exactly like a man and smoking those thin cigars, and Annie with her debutante mannerisms and wicked sense of humor.

Stroking her guest's hair, Violet sighed. It had been such a tragedy, Rebecca leaving for Boston, never to return, killed in a car accident. Soon afterwards, Annie had left too, taking the little girl.

Over the subsequent years, Violet had often wondered what became of them. At first she had received letters from Annie—strange disjointed ramblings. They were living with a married sister of hers, Violet recalled vaguely. After a few months, the letters had stopped coming. Eventually Violet had moved to Solarim for her retirement. It wasn't a glamorous life, but she had never been one for the bright lights.

With a sense of professional satisfaction, she probed the jagged cut on the girl's skull. After all these years, she still hadn't forgotten how to suture. She lifted an eyelid and shone her flashlight into the pupil. The patient had been swinging in and out of consciousness throughout the night. Apart from her head injuries, and a laceration to one thigh, she had survived her plane crash remarkably unscathed. It remained to be seen whether there was permanent brain damage. And, of course, it was always possible she could suffer a hemorrhage and never wake.

That would be dreadful, Violet thought. She was so much looking forward to having someone else to talk to for a change.

DEMORALIZED, CODY HOVERED over the radio set, willing it to burst into life. It was seven in the morning. By now, Annabel was either crawling out of Grace's bed after a night of torrid sex, or she was at the airport kicking her heels while Smithy tried to get the Dominie running.

If only they had normal telephone communications instead of a relic Alexander Graham Bell himself had probably constructed. They kept meaning to organize something more reasonable, but there were always other priorities. Such were the joys of life on a remote island in the South Pacific. Annabel had promised to look into cell phones, now that some of them had international range. It would save them having to fly to Rarotonga every time they wanted to call long distance.

Cody lifted her head, hearing something that might have been a cry. Intrigued by thrashing sounds coming from the foliage west of the villa, she reached the verandah in time to see a bedraggled figure emerge from the undergrowth. "Dawn! " Cody's jaw dropped.

The young woman was a sorry sight, clothes and skin stained luminous green, her face and hands filthy, and her hair a riot of leaves and flowers. Wearing a wide grin, she hobbled toward the verandah, heaved herself up the steps and collapsed into a wicker chair, demanding, "Well, aren't you going to offer me a drink?"

Flabbergasted, Cody retreated indoors and returned with a large glass of juice, handing it wordlessly to her visitor.

Between noisy gulps, Dawn announced, "I went to the Kopeka Cave. And I got sick from eating too many bananas. I tried to get here before dark, but I was bloody dying of pain. So I had to spend the night out there."

"You were out overnight?" Cody was mortified. How could she have been so negligent? Something might have happened to her...something obviously had.

The young woman was prattling happily, "I didn't think I could do it. You know, all that way by myself with my legs like this. Amazing, huh?"

"Yes," Cody affirmed weakly. "Incredible." She thought

about the Dawn of three years ago. Even in perfect health, she had made a production out of crossing the island on foot. "Why did you do it? I would have come and picked you up. All you had to do was call."

A little of Dawn's sparkle faded. "I'm not really sure. I mean I wanted to come see you, but I was kind of upset. I needed some time to think."

"About Grace?"

Dawn blushed beneath the grime. "I guess you know everything by now." She gave a small self-effacing laugh. "You must think it's just hilarious...after the way I've behaved all this time."

"I don't think that at all, Dawn," Cody said quietly.

"Well, I feel pretty stupid." Bitterness crept into Dawn's voice. "I know I didn't mean anything to Grace, but I guess I wanted—" The words wouldn't form and slow tears made rivulets in the dirt on her cheeks.

What did she want? Dawn wondered bleakly. Her feelings were in such disarray she had no idea. All she knew was that if Grace walked out of the jungle right now wearing that lopsided grin of hers, she would go weak at the knees with longing. She would drool like an idiot, blindly discard her self-respect and snatch whatever crumbs Grace chose to offer. How humiliating.

Cody was watching her with a sympathetic expression and Dawn felt even more abased, knowing how transparent she must seem. Jerking to her feet, she asked, "Can I use your shower?"

Cody followed her inside. "I'll get a change of clothes for you. I think you're about Annabel's size." Her voice caught as she said it, and Dawn gave her a second look.. Casting a glance in the direction of the radio, Cody explained in a tight voice, "Annabel didn't make it back from Raro yesterday. I guess she must be stuck there. She's always having fuel problems and stuff."

Dawn tried to control her expression. Annabel and Grace? Surely they wouldn't have run off together. No. Annabel might be fooling around a little, but she was far too classy to do a tacky thing like that. Dawn was relieved she hadn't given Cody that letter. It was not her place to interfere in someone else's relationship. If Cody and Annabel had problems, they would have to work them out like everybody else.

Cody was staring at her, eyes filled with trepidation. "Dawn? Is there something you want to tell me?"

Dawn felt uneasy. "Look, I really need that shower," she said, evasively.

"The shower can wait." Cody extracted a crumpled sheet of

paper from her shirt pocket and dropped it in Dawn's lap. Her face was grim. "I found this in your cottage."

"You went in my trash?" Dawn was horrified. No wonder Cody looked pale.

"Tell me everything," Cody said, her voice shaking slightly. "No bullshit, either."

# Chapter
## Twenty-one

GRACE'S HEART PUMPED, and her feet beat a steady tattoo on the concrete pathway. She veered onto a track that disappeared into the deep shadows thrown by a stand of firs. When the first man crossed her path, she paid no attention, skirting him to take the leafy track upward.

"Hey, what's the hurry?" he called after her, and Grace lengthened her stride a little.

In another few minutes she would reach open space again. She usually avoided this part of the park, but tonight she had a dinner date and the trees were a shortcut.

"Hey, babe. Got a light?" Another man emerged, blocking the narrow track.

"Sorry. Don't smoke." Grace detoured around a tree to avoid him. He blocked her path again, laughing softly. The odor of whiskey and sour tobacco sullied the green air.

Grace glanced sideways. The slope was steep, but she could make it down there through the trees and circle back. The road was close. Turning abruptly, she dodged the man, knees jarring as she made the rapid descent.

"Hey, guys," she heard. "She's all yours."

Someone grabbed at her. Thrown off balance she crashed heavily into a tree. Feeling a tearing sensation in her ankle, she reached for a low branch. Before she could get her footing, she was on the ground. Hot hands encircled her throat. Struggling, she watched three men emerge from the surrounding trees.

"Please," she croaked when the grip on her throat loosened. "Let me go and I won't make any trouble for you. C'mon guys, you've had your fun."

"Oh, no, we ain't." Mean dark eyes taunted her. "The fun's just beginning. Ain't that right, boys?"

Then Grace screamed. And screamed. And nobody heard her. Then she couldn't scream any more because they stuffed a strip of her T-shirt into her mouth.

Much later Grace felt something on her face, and smiled. A big soft yellow Labrador lay down beside her. Clouds swirled, dense and shapeless. There were voices. The dog was barking.

"Don't go," Grace begged it wordlessly. "Please don't leave me here."

Bells rang. A telephone.

Grace jerked bolt upright. Her sheets were soaked with sweat. She grabbed for the phone, shivering as the damp sheen evaporated from her skin.

It was Bevan, Annabel's pilot. They would be leaving for Moon Island in an hour.

Grace said she would be ready. Drained, she paced into the bathroom and touched her reflection in the mirror. When she could no longer bear to look, she stood beneath the torrid blast of the shower and soaped herself compulsively.


DAWN STOOD SLACK-JAWED beside Cody as the plane screeched to a halt and taxied along the pitted Moon Island strip. Painted khaki green, with a pinup girl embellishing the fuselage, it looked exactly like something out of an old war movie. As she and Cody drew closer, Dawn made out the words *Lonesome Lady* painted along the side. She stole an apprehensive glance at Cody.

"What the hell is this?" Cody asked as the pilot dropped to the ground in front of them.

Bevan Mitchell tucked his sunglasses into his top pocket and pulled out a packet of cigarettes. "She's a B-17 a genuine warbird."

Cody eyeballed him as though he were speaking in tongues. "Where's Annabel?" she demanded.

The pilot's eyes darted to the cockpit, and Dawn held her breath as Grace Ramsay emerged. Something in her expression made Dawn feel nauseated.

"You!" Cody gasped. "What the fuck are you doing here?"

Dawn grabbed at Cody's arm. She looked like she was going to take a swing at Grace.

Backing up, Grace said in a hurried voice. "Cody, we have some bad news." She shoved her hands into her pockets. "Annabel's missing."

"Missing?" The color fled Cody's face. "What do you mean, missing?"

"She left for Mitiaro Island yesterday," Bevan said. "She never arrived. There was a distress signal picked up three hundred miles southwest of Rarotonga about an hour and a half after she left."

"What does that mean?" Cody croaked. "Where is she?"

Bevan was visibly shaken. He crushed an unlit cigarette in his hand. "A search is underway. We'll be involved, of course. If you could get a few things together, we'll be on our way."

"I don't understand." Cody's tone rose sharply. "How can she be missing? Where's the Dominie?"

Instinctively Dawn took Cody's hand. She avoided Grace's piercing regard, hardened herself to the unspoken plea in the angle of her head, the nervous shift of her feet.

"Cody." Bevan spoke with palpable difficulty. "It's almost certain she's crashed. And because of the location it's going to be hard to spot the wreckage."

Cody gazed at him, stupefied.

"What do you mean about the location?" Dawn asked.

"It seems like she must have flown off-course somehow. The SOS coordinates would put her in an area where there is no land. Of course the signal may not have been hers."

"She went into the ocean?" Dawn whispered, stunned. That could only mean one thing. Annabel was dead.

Cody shook her head. "No!" she shouted, her face parchment white, eyes wild with shock. "It can't be true. I don't believe it!"


TWELVE HOURS LATER, Grace knocked on the door of Dawn's hotel room in Rarotonga. She felt hesitant, less than her usual assured self.

"What do you want?" Dawn asked her abruptly.

Grace took a couple of paces into the room. "Can we talk?"

"It's not a good time." Dawn hedged. "Cody might need me."

Grace glanced around. "Where is she?"

"Asleep in her room. The doctor gave her a sedative."

Unspoken words hung heavily between them. The search that afternoon had yielded nothing but an empty sea. Tomorrow they would resume at daybreak, across a wider radius. According to Bevan, there was almost no hope of locating her. Even if by some miracle she had survived a crash, she probably couldn't have lasted two days in the water.

Grace raised a hand to her eyes. For a moment she was sure she felt tears, but her fingers came back dry. "Poor Cody," she said, feeling a sob rise. Then she was numb again.

Dawn lifted bright accusing eyes. "What do you care?" she burst out.

"I care." Grace swallowed with difficulty. "Annabel and I were—"

"Yes, I know all about you and Annabel!" Dawn cut her short, lurching to her feet and cracking her walking stick viciously against the bed. "I know you were having an affair behind Cody's back, and so does she. If you say a word about it to her—" She whacked the bed again. "I'll flatten you."

In any other situation Grace would have laughed at the fierce threat. But the accusation momentarily stunned her. Dawn was glaring, chin tilted, and knuckles white.

"Dawn. I don't know what you're talking about," Grace said, perplexed. "Annabel and I aren't..."

Dawn promptly swung her stick in the air and thwacked it down at Grace's feet. "Liar!"

"Dawn!" Grace leapt out of the way. "Jesus Christ. Stop it!"

"No! You stop it!" Dawn shouted. "Stop lying to me. I saw you that night."

"What are you talking about? What night?"

Dawn flung her stick across the room. "You're disgusting," she said. "I don't know how you can be so dishonest. I mean, why bother lying now? Annabel is probably dead!"

Exasperated, Grace raked her fingers through her hair. "This is bizarre," she muttered. Striving for patience, she asked the infuriated young woman, "What exactly did you see and when?"

"It was the night after we...slept together the first time." Dawn's face was tight. "I wanted to see you and I hung around at home waiting forever, then I went to your place."

The night Annabel had come around to order her off the island. The night Grace told her about the rape. "You were there?" Grace asked. How much had Dawn heard?

"Yes, I was there." Dawn blazed. "Stupid gooey-eyed me. What an idiot." She pushed a balled fist roughly across her eyes. "And when I got there—"

"You saw me with Annabel on the verandah, and you added two and two and decided we were fooling around," Grace concluded on a hard note.

"Well, weren't you?"

"Jesus, Dawn." Obviously she hadn't overheard the conversation. She had just seen them holding one another and had drawn her own conclusions. Grace ran a weary hand across her forehead. She hardly knew where to begin. "Annabel and I are not lovers. We had a thing for a while, six years ago. Now we're just friends." And barely that, thanks to her job. "I was upset about something, that night. Annabel comforted me." Why was she explaining all this? Who cared what some silly kid wanted to believe?

Dawn rolled her eyes. "It looked like more than comfort to me."

Grace ordered herself to remain calm and virtuous, a credit to her Karate Sempei, to exercise self-control in the face of severe provocation, to demonstrate the spirit of perseverance. "Can I help it if you read all kinds of things into what you saw?" she shouted, failing on every count. "And what if we were involved? It's none of your goddamned business what I do!"

"Oh, I'm sorry," Dawn responded sarcastically. "Silly me. I forgot I'm not supposed to care. I forgot that it's all about meaningless sex."

"As I recall, you had no problem with that idea when I came round the next morning," Grace said with frigid irony. "I don't remember you asking me anything about Annabel. In fact, didn't we spend the entire day fucking?"

Dawn's face flushed brick red. "And that makes your behavior okay?"

"You know what I think," Grace threw at her, "I think you wanted me to stay. You didn't give a damn about me and Annabel then, did you? But because I left, I get...this shit."

The sulky fullness of Dawn's mouth grew more pronounced. Eyes welling with tears, she said in a small, husky voice, "You're right. I wanted you to choose me." She gave a forced half-laugh which failed to disguise the hurt. "Dumb, huh?"

An embarrassed silence followed. Grace's mouth felt dry. She wanted to offer Dawn something. An apology? For thoughtlessly inflicting hurt?. It was not her usual style to mess around with inexperienced kids who didn't know enough to keep the encounter in perspective. But it was a bit late for remorse now. Feeling like a heel, she backed toward the door. "I think I should go."

Dawn lifted disillusioned eyes. "Good idea."

# Chapter
## Twenty-two

THREE DAYS LATER, Annabel yawned and rearranged the cushions behind her head. "I still can't believe this," she told the silver-haired woman sitting opposite her.

"Fact is stranger than fiction, my dear," Violet Hazel pronounced. "How are you feeling this morning?"

"Terrific! I keep opening my eyes and wondering if I'm dead and this is just some kind of entrance exam for heaven." She lifted tentative fingers to explore the deep cut above her eyes. "That was some knock." Her head throbbed and her vision was blurred, but she was alive. Incredible.

Annabel glanced across at her companion. It was difficult to guess Violet Hazel's age—somewhere between sixty and eighty. Her face was creased and mobile, her eyes wonderfully blue.

Those eyes were the first thing Annabel had seen when she lifted her head the day before. Then there was the voice, warm and rounded. "Good morning, Lucy. Thanks for dropping by."

Annabel had decided immediately that she was in the presence of the Goddess herself. Who else could possibly have known the name she was born with? To double-check, she asked, "Where am I?"

"You're on Solarim Atoll," Violet Hazel informed her.

Solarim, an atoll so tiny it didn't even appear on most maps. Annabel was still astounded that she'd found it. Not only that, but she had survived to tell the tale. She smiled goofily.

Violet seemed amused. "I see you're still congratulating yourself on cheating the Grim Reaper."

"What can I say? I can't believe I'm here." Annabel thought about those final minutes, the odd calm that had descended when she was certain she was about to die. Naked in her emotional self, she had found a peace within thinking about Cody. If she had ever harbored any doubts about what mattered most in her life, she no longer did.

"People must be worried about me," she said. "My partner..." She hesitated, but sensed Violet Hazel was not a bigot. "Cody. She must be going crazy."

"Yes. Yes, of course." Violet's eyes registered Annabel's disclosure with a slight flicker of comprehension. "We must find a way to get word out. There's a Silk & Boyd freighter due soon. They always look in on me. I'll fire off a couple of flares, and they'll send someone in."

"You should have a radio."

Violet shrugged. "I'm not lonely."

"But you're very isolated. What if something happened and you needed help?"

"It did. I was awfully worried when I pulled you out of that plane."

"I was wondering how you got me here." Annabel said.

"On a stretcher. I dragged you along the sand."

Violet was nothing if not practical. Once a nurse on Rarotonga, the elderly woman still kept all manner of medical equipment in her home. And that was fortunate, Violet pointed out soon after Annabel gained consciousness. Both Annabel's leg and forehead had required stitches.

"I've been wondering." Violet poured tea into two china mugs. "Whatever were you doing out here in the first place?"

"I was flying to Mitiaro."

"But that's six hundred miles from here."

"Six hundred!" Annabel was stunned. How could she have gotten so far off course? "I had instrument failure. My compass wasn't working and neither was my fuel gauge."

"If you don't mind, I thought I might take a look at your plane this morning," Violet said. "Get her covered up."

Annabel's eyes started to sting. "I should come with you, but I don't think I can bear it." She pictured the Dominie, her sleek silver body mangled and smashed, skin torn to shreds. "The poor old thing. What an ignominious end for her."

"Hogwash," Violet said sternly. "She got you here, didn't she? If a machine has a spirit, hers will surely be rejoicing."

It was a bizarre notion, but curiously appealing. Annabel knew it was ludicrous to attribute human characteristics to a plane, but the Dominie felt like a friend. "I know it's crazy but I do feel like she saved my life," Annabel admitted. "I had no idea where I was going. It was almost like she steered me here."

"Then the least you can do is thank her," Violet declared imperiously.

Annabel's eyes widened. Her companion was quite serious. She was an old, eccentric woman, Annabel rationalized. It would be polite to humor her. Besides, Annabel was truly sad for the

Dominie, that gallant little plane, condemned to a flightless
future, rotting away on some unknown atoll.

Violet didn't wait for an answer. "C'mon. Up you get," she
said, gingerly placing a capacious straw hat on Annabel's head.
"Think you can walk a few yards at my pace?"

"I'm alive!" Annabel laughed. "I can do anything."

Violet handed her a large screwdriver. "Let's not get carried
away."


THE DOMINIE LAY burrowed into the sand at the opposite
end of the beach from Violet's cottage.

Once they had finished clearing out the surviving cargo,
Annabel turned her attention to the instruments. They were still
intact. She stared at the compass for a moment, glanced at the
sun, then called, "Violet? Which way is north?"

"That way." The white-haired woman pointed in the same
direction Annabel figured. Peering at the instrument panel, she
added, "Well, your compass wants to make a liar out of me,
doesn't it?" Her eyes flicked to Annabel's face.

"I should have trusted my instincts," Annabel said. Most
small plane crashes were caused by human error. Flying could be
very deceptive. Pilots were taught to trust their instruments.

Wielding a pair of bolt cutters, Violet clambered in to the
mangled nose of the plane. "Come and see this," she called after
a couple of minutes.

Annabel dangled over the instrument panel and peered into
the tangle of electronics. Violet had indicated the compass.
Detaching a small square of metal from the mounting, she passed
it up.

"It's a magnet," Annabel said, her mind spinning.

Violet nodded gravely. "Otherwise known as sabotage."

# Chapter
# Twenty-three

LEANING AGAINST THE hangar doorway, Grace watched cigarette smoke curl into Bevan's thinning blond hair. "Well, I guess that's it," she said, wearily removing her flying gear. Although they had conducted their search at low altitude, it still got icy cold in the B-17.

Bevan handed her a lit cigarette. "Maybe."

Grace glanced at him sharply. "You can't seriously think she's still alive."

He shook his head. "It's been a week. But stranger things have happened."

"Smithy says the plane would have gone straight to the bottom."

"That's what the Air Accident Report concludes. Odd it doesn't mention those filed flight plans."

"How could they have made such a mistake?" Grace took a puff on the cigarette, vowing she would not keep doing this. She hadn't smoked in years. Why start again now? "Someone wasn't doing his job. I can't understand why there's not some kind of inquiry."

"The guy responsible has resigned. They couldn't even locate him to get a statement."

"Wonderful. He takes his final paycheck and gets drunk. Annabel rots at the bottom of the Pacific."

"An' yer know somethin' else?" Smithy emerged from the hangar. "Me wife talked to 'er cousins on Mitiaro. They never 'eard of a medical emergency."

"But what about that Red Cross parcel?" Grace took a final drag and stubbed out the cigarette. "If there was no emergency, why did the hospital send it?"

The old man's eyes began to water. "Yer might well ask. Curse the day I fetched the bleedin' thing."

Bevan drew on his cigarette. "What exactly happened? Who told you there was an emergency?"

Smithy was shaking his head. "Air traffic phoned. 'Erself 'adn't arrived, so I nipped off an' picked it up to save 'er the trouble. The guy gives me the parcel and a new flight plan."

"They'd already prepared a new flight plan." Bevan remarked. "Amazing."

"What are you saying?" Grace surveyed him.

"I'm saying something doesn't sit right," Bevan responded. "No one in this place lifts a finger if they don't have to. But out of the goodness of his heart this controller prepared a flight plan and had it approved."

"Well, gawd a'mighty! I jes' remembered somethin'." Rattling around in his overall pockets, Smithy extracted a pair pliers and passed them across to Bevan. "Take a look at these, guvnor."

Bevan lifted an inquiring brow.

The wiry little man narrowed his eyes and spat to one side. "They was lying out there on the tarmac before she took off. I thought they was 'ers."


GRACE FOUND DAWN and Cody poolside at the hotel. This was Dawn's new strategy, intended to prevent Cody from spending every waking hour in her room, staring vacantly at the walls.

"Dawn? Can I speak with you?" Grace asked.

Bristling, Dawn glanced up from her Jackie Collins. She and Grace had barely spoken for the past three days, and that suited her fine. "What is it?" she said in a discouraging tone.

Sitting in the lounger next to Dawn's, Cody removed her sunglasses and looked up. "Is there some news?"

Grace squatted, eyes grave with the burden of bearing the same ill tidings day after day. "I'm sorry." It was how she began most conversations, of late. Today she had no map to lay out, no new search zones to discuss, no reports from the other craft, no spark of hope. "There's nothing new."

Cody sagged back, fidgeting absently with the curling jacket of her paperback. Sometimes she read a page, but mostly she simply stared into the book. Dawn knew her mind was elsewhere.

Grace flicked a brief glance toward Dawn and repeated her request. "Could we talk in private?"

Stubbornly disinterested, Dawn said, "Not right now."

Grace's expression registered disbelief, rapidly followed by exasperation.

Before she had a chance to respond, Cody said. "It's okay, Dawn. I feel like some time on my own anyway."

Grudgingly, Dawn tied a sarong over her bikini and accompanied Grace along the walkway past the hotel swimming pool to the lagoon. The beach gleamed with marble-fleshed tourists, earnestly absorbing the tanning rays of the tropical sun. Negotiating a sea of sunscreen bottles and coconut shells, the two women found a quiet spot near Arorangi village.

"Well?" Dawn said, avoiding Grace's eyes.

"The search is being scaled down," Grace informed her heavily. "We've done everything we can. Bevan is going to continue flyovers for the next few days, but it's a long shot."

Her shoulders sagged with defeat. Resisting an urge to hold her, Dawn said, "What are we going to tell Cody?"

"Cody's mom is arriving from New Zealand this morning," Grace replied. "She'll be staying here at the hotel. I thought maybe we'd wait 'til she gets here, then talk to Cody."

Dazed, Dawn fidgeted with the frayed cotton border of her sarong. "It doesn't feel real."

"I know." Grace fell silent for a moment. "I figured you and I would fly back to Moon Island this afternoon after Cody's been told."

"You and me. Why?"

"There's a lot to be done out there," Grace replied. "I was hoping you could stay on for a few days and lend a hand."

"Doing what?" Dawn gave her a frosty look.

Grace sighed. "Someone has to run the island. Mrs. Marsters has managed by herself for the last few days, but she's got a family. Look, I'm sorry I didn't discuss it sooner. I've been kind of busy."

Dawn was incredulous. "I don't know the first thing about running a tourist resort."

"You won't be by yourself. I can stay for a week or so."

"Aren't you supposed to be back in New York?" Dawn reminded her damply.

"I've taken vacation. Bevan and I have some loose ends to tie up..." She trailed off, vague all of a sudden.

Grace and Bevan. It sounded very cozy. Maybe there was another reason Grace was staying, Dawn thought. Maybe Grace was one of those lesbians like Cody's ex, Margaret, the woman who'd lived with Cody for five years, then left her for a man. Now she was living on some ashram in India, wearing a sari and making flower garlands for her guru. According to her last letter, she was pregnant, Cody had said. It didn't get much weirder than that.

Glowering at Grace, Dawn said, "I can run the island perfectly well by myself, thank you. I don't need your help."

"Come on, Dawn." Grace said impatiently. "You know that's absurd. You'd have to take the supplies around, either on horseback or driving the boat."

"And you don't think I can!" Dawn tossed her hair back. "Because I have a limp, I'm some kind of incompetent. Is that what you're saying?"

Grace groaned. "Be reasonable. Moon Island is a two-person job. Cody's too depressed to do anything, right now. Can't we just agree to put our differences aside for a few days. Surely it's the least we can do for Cody...and Annabel."

"Oh, now you care about them?"

"Don't push it," Grace's mouth thinned. "By the way, did you tell Cody you made a mistake?"

Dawn's shoulders tightened. "I told her I got the wrong end of the stick, and I should have known better."

"Thank you," Grace said.

Her look of injured dignity made Dawn irrationally angry. "I'll help," she said, giving her a scathing look. "So long as you stay out of my way, okay?"

"Okay. Whatever." Grace's tone bordered on meekness, but her flinty eyes were anything but docile.

Avoiding them, Dawn looked quickly away. Her traitorous heart hammered against her chest, shameless as always in its response to Grace. Ignoring it's wayward entreaties, Dawn said, "Have reception page me when it's time to go," and walked away without glancing back."


"IT'S HARD TO accept that someone wants to kill me," Annabel said. "I haven't done anything."

"Perhaps it's somebody's idea of a joke," Violet said. "Nothing would surprise me."

"Violet! That's so cynical."

"My dear, at my age one cannot afford to harbor trite illusions about the nature of the human condition. The shock of disillusionment could prove fatal."

Annabel raised her hand to the wound on her forehead. The stitches pulled a little. "I think we can rule out the joke idea. But I can't think of anyone I've wronged so badly they would want to kill me. One would hope to notice that kind of enemy."

"I'm certain you would, my dear. Revenge is an act of powerful emotion. Most victims have some kind of relationship with their killers. When you think about it, suicide is just revenge turned inward. Such an intimate crime."

"Well, I definitely didn't plant the damned magnet myself,"

Annabel said. "And there's that Red Cross parcel. It was empty, remember."

"Indeed." Violet's expression was pensive. "So who would have something to gain by killing you? Who finds you a threat or an obstacle?"

Annabel hesitated. "It's crazy. But there is one person."

By the time Annabel had finished describing Robert Hausmann's bid to buy the island, his plans to use it for toxic waste dumping, and his hints that the Cook Islands government might have been involved in insider trading, Violet was looking smugly convinced.

"That's your man, Annabel. He's ruthless, greedy, and unethical."

Annabel laughed. "You just described most of the so-called civilized world!"

"Why do you think I live out here?"

"How long have you been on Solarim?"

Violet gave that some thought. "I've been in the Cook Islands for more than forty years," she pronounced. "I stayed on Raro until the seventies. Then the government said I could live here. They pay me, you know—I'm rather like a lighthouse keeper, only without a lighthouse."

"That's why you have the generator and the lights on the roof? In case there's a ship in distress out there?"

"It hasn't happened yet," Violet said. "But if it ever does I have ropes, life jackets, and an inflatable in the shed."

Annabel laughed. "You're a feisty woman, Violet." She was struck by a thought. If Violet had been in the Cook Islands for forty years, and if she had recognized Annabel was Lucy, she must have known Aunt Annie quite well. Yet she hadn't said anything when Annabel mentioned that she had inherited the island. Annabel had the impression she was biding her time, waiting until Annabel had regained strength.

"Did you ever visit Moon Island?"

"Several times." Violet's eyes creased with pleasure. "I think it's the most beautiful island in the whole Pacific. It's even lovelier than Aitutaki."

"I think so too." Suddenly Annabel felt like crying. She could almost see the moon suspended over Passion Bay, smell the late-night heaviness of frangipani and gardenia. She pictured Cody sitting alone on their verandah, waiting for her.

"There, there ..." Violet pulled her into the present with a pat on the hand. "I knew, the moment I saw you, that you were Lucy Adams."

Annabel sat very still. "You knew me back then?"

Violet promptly went inside the house and returned with a battered old photo album. "Oh, yes. Just look at this."

She singled out a fading photo, then another and another, until Annabel's eyes flooded and she could no longer read the captions. Annie and Rebecca gazed out at her from a sepia past, speaking to her heart after thirty silent years.

"You're Lucy, aren't you?" Violet said.

Annabel could only nod dumbly. Her throat was too constricted for words.

"You were the most beautiful child I've ever seen. Rebecca was just mad over you. Look." She flipped the page and Annabel was staring at a woman with short black hair and brooding eyes. She stood slouched against a tree trunk, wearing men's pants, one hand casually stuffed in a pocket, the other holding a tiny fair-haired child aloft. Lucy. Herself as a toddler.

"I remember that day still." Violet's voice shook slightly. "It was the day Rebecca left on the freighter to visit her family in America. She never came back." She dabbed at her eyes with a flimsy handkerchief. "Look at me. All sentimental."

"Oh, Violet. This means so much to me. You have no idea." Annabel was laughing and crying at the same time. "I can't believe this is happening. I must have been meant to come here. It was my destiny."

"It most certainly wasn't," Violet reminded her. "It was attempted murder, and we shall see the scoundrel responsible is brought to justice. Mark my words."

Annabel smiled. "That wasn't what I meant. But you know that, don't you? You're just teasing."

Violet lifted her eyebrows. "I'm very serious indeed, young woman. The freighter gets here tomorrow. It only comes once a month, you know, and if we're going to catch it, we've got work to do."

"Yes ma'am." Annabel immediately wiped her tears and sat up straighter in her chair.

Violet gave an approving nod. "But before we start, tell me, is your mother still alive?"

"Annie died three years ago. It's rather a long story, I'm afraid."

Violet's eyes crinkled. "Fortunately time is a blessing here, not a curse."

Annabel gave her a grateful smile. "Well, for a start, I didn't know I was Annie's daughter. Her sister Laura adopted me, you see, and renamed me Annabel Worth. After Rebecca died, Annie went back home to Boston and—"

"Oh this is going to be a long story," Violet interrupted,

squeezing Annabel's hand. "Why don't I fetch some fresh tea and biscuits before it becomes truly gripping."

# Chapter
# Twenty-four

"IT'S BRILLIANT." GRACE dropped a sheaf of neatly typed pages onto the table. "Right on the jugular."

"The very least the bastard deserves." Bevan passed a freshly lit cigarette to a thin, dark-haired man beside him.

Don Jarvis took a contemplative drag. "*Time* will go for it. Business ethics is hot."

"Where did you dredge up all that stuff?" Grace asked.

Don quirked an eyebrow. "A guy like Hausmann makes a few enemies on his way up the ladder."

"Do you think we've got enough for the Cook Island's police to go on?"

"If the government didn't pay their salaries, maybe, " Bevan said.

"You mean they won't arrest him?" Grace was astounded.

"They can't. The government has too much to lose. They're in shit to their eyeballs, sweetheart. This place can't afford another Albert Henry."

"He was the Premier who got sacked for corruption, right?"

"It's not often Queen Elizabeth kicks ass." Don grinned. "Brought down the government."

"There must be some way..." Grace could hardly take it in. "A woman is dead because they were looking to make a fast buck. We owe her some justice, don't we?"

"Grace, she wouldn't want it." Bevan stubbed out his cigarette. "She loved these islands. Have you any idea how much a public scandal like this would shame the local people?"

"You're talking about murder!" Grace gasped. "You're saying Hausmann stays out of jail so that a bunch of corrupt bureaucrats can keep their jobs and the public can keep their illusions. That stinks."

"That's politics," Don said bluntly. He leafed through his article. "Look, I've turned up enough dirt on Hausmann to bury the guy. When this hits the press back home, the IRS will be all over Argus like a biblical plague. The SEC will slap an injunction on them so fast Hausmann won't know which way is up. They've been on his tail for years. The guy will definitely serve time."

"But not for murder." Grace cradled her head in her hands. Without either the plane or Annabel's body, they couldn't prove there had actually been a murder. All they had was suspicion and circumstantial evidence. And Bevan had a point. The last thing Annabel would want is for the Cook Islands to be pilloried in the international press, thrown into political turmoil, their fragile economy shattered. It was so unjust.

"It's not fair," she whispered. Her guts churned. No one ever paid for the hurt they inflicted. There were four men roaming free out there who had sentenced her to years of emotional isolation.

"It won't bring her back, Grace." Bevan dropped an arm over her shoulders. "Revenge doesn't work that way."


DAWN WASN'T AT Villa Luna when Grace returned. She prowled the house, fatigue vying with a sharp disappointment. Since their arrival on Moon Island, communication with Dawn had been polite and distant. They slept in rooms at opposite ends of the villa, ate meals together, and conducted the business of the resort with impersonal diligence.

Dawn was always busy with something and gave the impression that interruption was not welcome. Most often she took refuge in the garden, weeding and trimming. Sometimes she would be on the telephone chatting with a guest, and Grace would eavesdrop for a moment, resentment gnawing at her. Dawn sounded so warm when she spoke to everyone else.

It was crazy to give a damn and Grace could not afford the time to be small-minded. Along with her responsibilities at the resort, she had poured hours into the investigation of Annabel's disappearance. Determined to follow up suspicions of foul play, Bevan had enlisted his lover, Don, a freelance journalist, to sleuth around. What they uncovered had been even more shocking than they expected.

An unidentified man in overalls had been seen leaving the Dominie's hangar the afternoon Annabel set off for Mitiaro. An Air Traffic Controller had resigned that day and was known to have departed for New Zealand with unseemly haste and a lot of money. It also seemed clear that someone high in the ranks of officialdom was doing his best to obstruct inquiries around the accident—a classic cover-up, Don said.

Taking the familiar track from Villa Luna to Passion Bay,

Grace tried to convince herself that Don's exposé feature would damage to Hausmann enough to serve justice. Her boss would lose everything that really mattered to him—reputation, career, money.

But all Grace could think about was Annabel. How she had been robbed of the happiness it had taken her so long to find, how much she had loved Moon Island and what that love had cost her.

Again the enormity of Hausmann's actions struck her. Environmental destruction was one thing, but murder? Reflecting uneasily on the ethics of both, Grace paused to disentangle herself from a sticky creeper overhanging the track. In some ways there was a logical progression. Numerous deaths had been caused through the disposal of toxic waste—was that murder? No, that was negative publicity. And Annabel? Why was that situation different? Because her death was more immediate, more personal? Because she was a wealthy, beautiful white woman?

Shoving her hands into her pockets, Grace crossed the hot sand to stand over a lissom form reclining on a pink towel.

Dawn lifted the brim of her hat and blinked against the glare of the sun. "Oh, it's you." Her bathing suit, no thicker than a coat of paint, was a reluctant concession to Grace's intrusive presence at Villa Luna. It revealed far more than it covered.

A hot rush of lust made her nipples harden. She should leave and give Dawn her space, Grace told herself.

Kicking off her sandals, Grace lowered herself to the sand. She recognized Dawn's expression. Wariness and determined indifference. Who could blame her? Grace cast a wry sideways glance at her companion. Dawn's attention was on yet another Jackie Collins novel. Pointedly, she ignored the not quite accidental brush of Grace's thigh against hers.

Memories clawed at Grace, and she felt a wrenching sense of loss. She had alienated the only woman who had evoked real emotion in her since the attack, and she had no idea how to undo the damage.

After a few minutes' silence, Dawn lifted her eyes from the paperback, her irritation barely concealed. "Did you want something?"

"Just your company," Grace said.

Dawn shrugged. "Feel free." Flipping open the top of her sunscreen bottle, she methodically plastered her legs.

The scar tissue looked very sensitive. She remembered seeing Dawn for the first time, her legs pale and wasted, scars knitting flesh torn by injuries too horrible to contemplate. How had it happened? What terror did she revisit alone at night? Grace stretched out her hand and touched a long white mark. "Tell me about the accident," she said.

Flinching, Dawn brushed Grace's fingers away as she might an insect. "I told you. It was a car accident," she replied flatly.

"How did it happen?"

"Look, do we have to discuss this? I was knocked out. I don't remember anything much. One minute I was driving, the next minute I was in hospital."

"Do you ever have nightmares about it?"

Dawn turned sharply, as though Grace were about to humiliate her with some unsuspected sleep-time indiscretion. "No. But you do."

Grace waited a beat. "Not any more. I had one last week and since then...nothing. I'm not sure if I'll have that dream again."

Dawn sat up, shaking the sand from her hair. "What makes you think so?"

Grace contemplated five years of waking in a sweat almost every night, of working so late she could barely keep her eyes open, in the hopes she might sleep the unbroken sleep of exhaustion. "Because I think some dreams are messages from our subconscious, and they keep on repeating until we're ready to hear them."

"And now that you've heard yours, the nightmare will stop?"

"I hope so." Wrapping her arms around her knees, Grace leaned forward and stared out to sea. Was that how it worked? Was the conscious mind little more than a gatekeeper to the subconscious? Did dreams unlock doors to secrets housed within? She had concealed four faces there, the assailants she could not identify to the police. In protecting herself from the reality of her rape, she had protected her rapists, too.

"Well, it sounds like a pretty complicated way of finding out something you already know." Dawn gathered her beach paraphernalia and brushed herself off. Apparently she'd had her fill of Grace's company.

Longing to detach herself from her newly awakened memories, Grace stared out to sea. She felt terribly alone. The thought of returning to New York and picking up life where she'd left off seemed almost ridiculous. But what was the alternative? Grace shook herself mentally. She was far away in a beautiful place, caught up in the midst of dramatic events. She had enjoyed a holiday fling with a sexy young woman, and even if their brief passionate interlude was history, Grace still liked being around her. It all added up to one thing—escapism.

"Are you in for dinner?" Dawn's voice, cool and polite,

intruded on her musings.

"I'll fix myself something when I get back," Grace said.

With measured movements, Dawn stood and shook out her towel. Her legs looked stronger, Grace thought. The wasted muscles were toning up again. Spared the daily dose of harsh swimming pool chemicals, her hair fell in a heavy curtain of honeyed silver.

"You're looking good, Dawn," Grace remarked.

Dawn's voice softened. "Grace," she ventured after a pause, "are you okay?"

"I—" Grace shrugged helplessly. A huge sob rose in her chest. She lifted a hand to her face, startled to find it wet. Uncontrollable emotion welled, and she scrambled to her feet. "I'll talk to you later," she said and half ran down the beach toward the sea.

Halting where the tide stirred the fine sand into whirling eddies, she keeled over, retching violently. She could not stop shaking. Unable to stand, she sank down onto her knees, tears streaming down her face.

When Dawn's arms closed around her, she offered no resistance. Allowing herself to be held, Grace surrendered to a grief too profound to face alone any more.


SEVERAL HOURS LATER, Dawn tilted her head to face the woman beside her. Grace had cried in Dawn's arms for what seemed an eternity, first on the beach, then in bed after Dawn brought her back to the cottage. Like a child, Grace had allowed herself to be bathed and comforted. Now, finally, her sobs had subsided and her breathing was normal again.

Dawn stroked her cheek tentatively, and Grace's eyes opened. "Hello," Grace murmured.

There was a softness about her expression that Dawn had never seen. And something else, something that seemed meant for her alone. Dawn swallowed painfully. She was almost afraid to hold that steady gaze, afraid that at any moment the tenderness would forsake that mouth, and cool, cynical Grace Ramsay would stare back at her.

Instead Grace's voice was gentle. Her hand found Dawn's. "Can you forgive me?"

"For what?" Dawn hardly dared breathe.

"For everything. I've treated you badly. I want to make it up to you."

Dawn blushed. She slid her fingers between Grace's, and for a long moment they stared at one another. Then Grace kissed her slowly and tenderly on the mouth.

If only she could freeze time, Dawn thought. If she could just seize this single, magical moment before it fell prisoner to the inevitable. Spellbound, she opened her eyes. Love. It declared itself in siren promises, blazed like sunlight behind closed eyes, painted the air between them. Love. She had thought she would never know that feeling, that she might fail to recognize it. She almost laughed.

Grace caressed Dawn's cheek, cupping its baby fullness in her hand, and stretching her fingers to coil a honey-silver strand of hair. With amazement, she saw that her fingers were shaking. The cynical Grace seemed oddly disengaged. *You're going to make a fool of yourself,* a voice in her head warned. Yet when her eyes locked with Dawn's, she no longer heard the white noise of her own doubts. There was only silence, perfect and complete. Placing a hand to Dawn's chest, she felt the steady beat of her heart, took Dawn's hand and held it between her own breasts.

"We're in time," Dawn whispered and Grace held her, frightened to speak, to move, in case she destroyed the fragile new bond between them.

# Chapter
## Twenty-five

DAWN TOUCHED CODY'S elbow. "Let's take a walk on Passion Bay. It's time you got out of the house."

Cody shook her head, barely responding.

Dawn fidgeted. "Would you like something to eat?"

Another shake of the head.

"You really should. You're looking ill."

Cody shrugged listlessly. "I'm not hungry." Her shoulders sagged, and she pushed her fingers back through her short, dark hair. "I can't believe it," she said softly.

"Cody..." Dawn stretched an impulsive arm, but Cody shied away.

Over the past few days, Cody had grown disturbingly remote, avoiding touch, and seldom speaking. At her mother's suggeston, she had returned to Moon Island while arrangements were being made for Annabel's memorial service. Now Dawn wasn't sure if this had been such a good idea. All Cody did was sit on the verandah and stare out to sea.

People handle shock and grief in their own ways, Grace said. But Dawn couldn't bear it. She was desperate to find some way to offer comfort. "I'll make us a cup of tea," she said and limped into the house.

She wished Grace were here. Grace seemed to know what to do when Cody forgot to go to bed or brush her hair. She'd been through something like it herself once, she'd said in an offhand tone that meant she didn't plan on saying any more.

As Dawn arranged a teapot and cups on a tray her thoughts strayed to Grace. Since that afternoon of weeping, she had been so gentle and kind. They went walking and swimming together, talked for hours about Dawn's accident and her plans for the future. Grace helped with her exercise program, pushing her harder than she might have pushed herself.

Yet Dawn felt she hardly knew her. Grace seldom talked about herself. She chatted easily about places she had been and things she had done, told amusing anecdotes about life in New York City. But she shied away from personal questions.

Dawn had extracted the information that she had a married sister in New Orleans and her English parents had retired to Miami Beach. Her family knew she was a lesbian, and it didn't seem to be a problem. Grace had a small apartment somewhere called the West Village. She lived by herself. It was easier, Grace said without explaining why.

At times Dawn longed to ask her what it was she wasn't saying—what it was that had made her break down that day. Grace gave the impression of being open and candid, yet Dawn was conscious that something was always held back. At times she wondered if it was her imagination. Physically, Grace was affectionate and warm. They held hands and hugged like close friends. Yet they did not make love.

Dawn told herself it was because of the tragedy they were all dealing with in their different ways, and she felt ashamed of her own yearnings. Sometimes she just wanted the old flirtatious Grace back. She wanted to be thrown onto her bed. She wanted Grace to rip off her clothes and for them to make love for hours.

She couldn't understand why they weren't sleeping together. She had made it obvious that she wanted to, but Grace just didn't seem interested. Maybe she wasn't attracted to her that way anymore, Dawn thought miserably. Maybe Grace had found her fun for a couple of nights, but had no enduring sexual interest in her.

She wished she had someone to talk to about it, but there was only Cody, and under the circumstances, it was hardly an appropriate conversation topic. How could she think about having sex at a time like this anyway? Full of self-reproach, she lifted the tray, balancing it carefully to compensate for her halting stride.

Cody was staring across Passion Bay with such attuned concentration, even Dawn found herself listening for the strangled hum of the Dominie, scanning the horizon for a glint of silver. It still felt unreal to know that Annabel would never come back again.

She offered a bone china cup to Cody, releasing a gasp of shock as it was knocked abruptly from her hand. "Cody!"

The boyish figure was already kneeling beside the shattered pieces, shoulders hunched. "I'm sorry," Cody whispered.

Dawn sprang down beside her. "It's okay. It doesn't matter."

"These are Annabel's favorites." Cody looked up at Dawn. "It's tomorrow, isn't it?" Her eyes were dark with pain.

The memorial service. Dawn nodded mutely.

"I can't believe it," Cody whispered. Then she was on her feet, hurling the broken pieces down with a viciousness that sent the mynah birds fleeing from their hopeful sentinel along the verandah railing. "I can't believe it. I can't! I can't!" She paced the verandah, shaking her head. "Why?" she suddenly shouted at Dawn. "Why did it have to be her? Of all the creeps out there who fucking deserve to die, why her? Oh God, I can't bear it. She can't be dead. She's not dead!"

Dawn started to cry. She couldn't believe it either. There was a bizarre unreality about this whole experience. It felt like television. She almost expected to wake up and discover that none of this was really happening. She was not the Dawn Beaumont who had gone on holiday and fallen in love with a woman who didn't want her. Annabel had not crashed her plane. Cody was not acting like a madwoman.

"They haven't even found the plane. So how do they know she's dead?" Cody's pacing turned to stomping. "The whole thing was a shambles. Why didn't they look for her when they got the distress call? It's their fault. And now she's gone. She's gone!" The final word was a wild sob, then Cody was repeating the phrase over and over, weeping brokenly.


ANNABEL'S MEMORIAL SERVICE was held in the gardens at Arorangi. It looked like everyone on Rarotonga was there with the devout islanders in their church finery. The early nineteenth-century missionaries, who had taken over the Cook Islands, had attempted to ban dancing, flowers, and anything else that looked like fun. But the islanders weren't buying it, apparently convinced that the dour extremes of Protestant abstemiousness were best left to those fool enough to wear starched underclothes in the tropics.

Annabel's family was planning a ceremony back in Boston. They were on their way to Rarotonga to take Cody back with them. It wouldn't be anything like this, Dawn figured. There wouldn't be hundreds of people wearing flowers and crying noisily. There wouldn't be guitars and the biggest feast she had ever seen.

It was weird listening to a eulogy when there was no body to bury. Her attention strayed to Grace, then swung back to the preacher who was leading the service. A big silver-haired man in an ornate robe, he waved his arms a lot as he spoke. His sermon was in English and Maori, the two completely dissimilar languages fusing resonantly as he spoke.

Cody sat between Dawn and Bevan. Further along the pew were the Premier and various dignitaries. Obviously Annabel had been someone important in this community. The preacher strode back and forth, pausing to direct comments to Cody.

Dawn had difficulty following everything he said. He seemed to be talking about Moon Island and the various legends connected with it. Dawn supposed it was all just superstition, but she was fascinated anyway.

To the early inhabitants of Rarotonga, Moon Island was considered sacred to several goddesses. Legend had it that if men ever occupied the island, these goddesses would be angry, and no more children would be born to the Cook Islanders. This pronouncement seemed to generate considerable shuffling among the ranks of the dignitaries. The specter of infertility got the islanders pretty worked up, given they weren't supposed to pay any heed to such idolatrous superstition.

"But we are blessed," the preacher declared, then added as something of an afterthought, "by the Lord." He waited for the devout to say amen. "We were sent two daughters to safeguard the island for our people."

Everyone clapped. Dawn was bewildered. This wasn't like any funeral she'd ever attended.

"But one daughter could only stay for a short time. And in that time she made many gifts to our people." This comment led to a flurry of fanning and sobbing. "Our daughter Annabel has gone," the preacher intoned. "May the Lord grant her eternal rest." Feverish amens. "But our daughter Cody remains." Audible sighs of relief. "We weep with her at the loss of a loved one."

The crying was contagious. Dawn couldn't stop herself. She blubbered noisily into her handkerchief, squeezing Grace's hand until her fingers went weak. Then a very strange thing happened. Cody got up as though she were in a trance and turned to face the congregation, her face startled, expectant.

An awed hush fell, and like the islanders, Dawn found herself craning in the direction Cody was staring, trying to see what it was she was seeing.

"Annabel?" Cody's whisper radiated into the hush.

The preacher tried to keep things in line. "Her spirit is with us."

Dawn's spine tingled. She could almost believe it.

Then a voice at the rear of the gathering said, "So is her body." Accompanied by an old woman in very peculiar clothing, Annabel walked calmly through the throng and straight up to her lover, just in time to catch her as she fainted.

In the heady chaos that ensued, Dawn didn't know whether

she was laughing or crying. There were people on their knees praying, others singing and clapping, the smell of food cooking. Annabel was all but buried in flowers and joked about being smothered to death. Beside her, Cody looked flushed and dazed.

"It's a miracle," Dawn declared breathlessly and gazed around for Grace in the milling crowd. She was nowhere to be seen. Jumping into the fray, Dawn elbowed her way over to Annabel and Cody. "Have you seen Grace?" she demanded as the two women caught hold of her.

Annabel scanned the faces around them. "She was here a minute ago talking with Bevan."

Dawn frowned. Grace was always off talking to Bevan. A man.

"She'll be back." Annabel smiled and gave her a squeeze. "Come with us and have something to eat."

Dawn's mouth watered at the prospect, but she wanted Grace. She wanted her right now. "I'll go and have a look for her first."

As Dawn turned to leave, Annabel caught her arm. "I almost forgot. I've got something for you. It's been sweated on and bled on and very nearly died on." She produced a crumpled note. "Grace asked me to give this to you the day all this started. It seemed important, so I kept it for you."

Dawn unfolded the note and stared at its contents: a New York address and phone number and some scrawled words.

*I lied. You do matter to me and I need to see you again. Please phone me. Grace*

Conscious she was starting to blush, Dawn stashed the folded paper in her pocket, kissed Annabel gratefully on the cheek, and hustled her way into the crowd.

Grace was nowhere to be found, and neither was Bevan. The more she hunted, the more frustrated she grew. Why weren't they here? This was Annabel's wake-turned-welcome-home party. What could they possibly be doing that was more important?

A nasty suspicion fluttered across her mind. Grace and Bevan? No. It couldn't be possible. They'd only been spending time together because they were involved in the search for Annabel. Well, she was back now. So where the hell were they?

Dawn was fuming when she stumbled on Smithy, who was drinking beer a few yards from the crowd. She tugged on his arm. "Have you seen Grace and Bevan?"

He looked startled, then faintly sheepish.

"It's important." Dawn was almost hopping from one foot to the other.

Smithy cleared his throat. "The guvnor did mention something about the hangar, Miss. But he said..."

Dawn didn't wait for him to finish. Bolting off in the direction of Main Street, she hitched a ride to the airport on the first minibus she spotted.

# Chapter
# Twenty-six

"HOW LONG HAVE you been with Don?" Grace asked as Bevan twisted segments of wire together with his pliers.

"Eight years."

"You're not fed up with one another?"

"Quite the opposite."

Grace smiled wryly. She could believe it. She'd spent enough time around Don and Bevan to sense they were the male equivalent of Cody and Annabel. "You mean the novelty still hasn't worn off?"

"Novelty was never really the attraction. We'd both had enough of that for one lifetime."

Grace made a fuss of the knots she was working on. "You're quite a bit older than Don, aren't you?"

"About the same difference as you and Dawn." Bevan returned Grace's sharp look with an unrepentant grin. "You don't take too many chances, do you, Grace?"

"Only the kind that pay off."

"Life must be very predictable."

"I like it that way."

"Then I guess you'll be heading back home soon?"

She nodded stiffly. "In a couple of days' time."

Taking a few paces back, Bevan studied their masterpiece. "Well, what do you think?"

Grace fell in beside him, her gaze encompassing the B-17 which was festooned from nose to tail with tropical flowers and a huge pink bow twelve o'clock high. "I'll be honest with you Bevan. I think we could have saved ourselves a lot of trouble and just put a sack over its nose. Annabel would still kiss the propeller tips."

"Yeah, that's Annabel. No bullshit about her priorities."

"Why am I feeling got at all of a sudden?" Grace politely inquired.

Bevan lobbed a hard look in her direction. "What do you want, Grace? You want me to let you off the hook when you put yourself up there in the first place?"

"Well, thanks. You're a real friend."

"Someone has to be."

Grace was stung. "I gather this touching concern is all on account of Dawn Beaumont. I suppose it wouldn't occur to anyone that maybe I'm not setting out to break her heart."

Bevan raised an eyebrow. "You weren't listening, were you?"

"I'm not used to a man telling me how to run my life."

"I'm not used to giving a damn if some mate of my boss's wants to shoot herself in the foot."

Grace's cheeks stung as if they'd been slapped. A man was calling her an emotional cripple. "Jesus, where do you couple-cultists get off?" she tossed at him. "Wise up, Bevan. Some of us aren't looking to be recruited."

"Sure, Grace. My mistake."

Grace slammed her pliers onto the workbench. "Let's go get everyone. We're late for a party."

At Bevan's watchful silence, her anger faded. The two of them had been through some rough times, scouring the ocean for a glimpse of wreckage, trying to raise one another's spirits when all hope had gone. Impulsively, she tucked her arm into his. "Don't worry about me," she said. "It's nice of you, but I'll be okay, really."

Bevan met her eyes. "What about Dawn?"

"Yes, what about Dawn?" A small, cross voice carried across the airy hanger.

Grace caught her breath and turned slowly. Dawn was staring from her to Bevan, eyes full of accusation.

Bevan, yellow-gutted, wasted no time. "What say I go and pick up Annabel and Cody?"

"Be my guest," Dawn told him, hands on hips. Surveying him belligerently, she added, "And don't go getting any ideas about Grace. She's a lesbian."

"Dawn!" Grace stared after Bevan's retreating figure and tried to stifle her laughter. But it came out anyway, in a thin hysterical wheeze.

"What's so funny?" Dawn demanded. "You go off with some man in the middle of the party and come out here to... to..."

"Dawn, Bevan's gay."

Dawn's jaw dropped.

Grace tried not to laugh. "It's true. Don's his lover."

Dawn's cheeks reddened. "How was I supposed to know? No one ever tells me anything." She noticed the bomber. "Why has that plane got flowers and bows all over it?"

"Because it's a coming-home present for Annabel."

"From Bevan?"

"Sort of. And guess what—they're not having an affair, either."

"Oh, ha ha. Very funny." Dawn pouted.

"He's giving her half ownership. We just thought we'd pile on the glitz."

"I see." Dawn's mouth formed a small, round pucker. Grace wanted to kiss her.

"Annabel gave me this." The young woman shyly held up a dog-eared note. "I... It means a lot to me."

"I couldn't just leave like that," Grace admitted. "I thought I could, but fortunately there are limits even to my stupidity."

Staring at Dawn's upturned face, Grace felt humbled. The young woman's expression was so revealing—hopeful, a little indignant, way too vulnerable. Grace slid her arms around Dawn's waist and drew her close, planting a tender kiss on her forehead. The silence between them stretched into one of those unexpected and glorious moments when happiness seems there for the asking. Words fluttered precariously.

"Dawn," Grace began. "I—"

A loud honking reverberated around the hangar, and both women turned in startled dismay. Bevan's jeep blocked the doorway. Out of it piled half a dozen people: Bevan and Don, Smithy, Cody, the indomitable Violet. They led Annabel, blindfolded and making laughing complaints, across the hangar.

"What is this?" Annabel protested. "Plucked from the jaws of death, and now I'm kidnapped!"

Bevan faced her toward the B-17 and removed the blindfold.

Annabel looked completely stunned. Flushing dark crimson, she stumbled toward the bomber. "Oh my God, a B-17," she whispered. A radiant smile lit her face. "How on earth did you lay your hands on this?"

"I got lucky."

Annabel circled the nose, gazing up at the Plexiglass. "I thought there were none left."

"She's one of a handful. There's a few still in service in the States. They use them for firebombing. And there's a couple in Europe. I saw Sally B while I was back home."

Staring up at the Vargas Girl painted on the fuselage, Annabel read, "Lonesome Lady."

"One of my uncles rebuilt her after the war," Bevan said. "She's been gathering dust on his farm ever since."

"And he's given her to you?" Annabel beamed. "That's fantastic!"

Bevan handed her a sheaf of papers. "Take a look."

Annabel flicked through the ownership documents, then fell silent for a moment. "She's registered in both our names," she said huskily.

Bevan offered his arm. "Want a tour of your plane?"

Smithy propped a ladder against the fuselage and opened the cockpit door.

Beaming, Annabel turned to Cody. "Isn't she wonderful!"

Cody's smile was blended with gloom. "Decent seats would be a bonus."

"Seats!" Smithy snorted. "Yer talkin' about a bomber, girl. C'mon." He cocked his head at Dawn, Grace and Don. "You lot can climb in 'er tail."

Dawn hung back a little. "You mean this plane was really in the war?"

"Got the flak marks to prove it." Smithy opened the rear door. "This old girl flew eight missions to Big B, an' she got 'ome every time."

"It dropped bombs on people?" Dawn asked. What was it with men and their war fetish?

"Enemy targets," Smithy rasped.

Eyeing the gun turrets, Dawn felt even more squeamish.

Annabel stuck her head out the cockpit door. "Let's take her up, Smithy."

"C'mon baby." Grace lifted Dawn up to Cody, who was hanging out of the tail wearing a fleecy jacket. "I'll give Smithy a hand, then I'll fight you for the ball turret."

They towed the B-17 out onto the tarmac. Grace chocked the wheels while Smithy radioed for clearance.

"Delay," he relayed to Annabel with an expressive scowl. "Some millionaire in a bloody private jet."

"My God." Grace recognized the Argus logo. "It's Hausmann." She swung herself into the rear door and plunged along the B-17's tail to the radio room. "Hausmann's here," she told Don.

Don was silent for a moment, his brow creased. "Think you can get the asshole aboard?"

"Before I break his face, or after?"

Pushing past Dawn and Cody, Grace bailed out, shouted to Smithy to wait, and pounded off across the tarmac.


"WE'LL ALL BE arrested for this," Dawn muttered two hours later as Grace and Don frog-marched Robert Hausmann up the steps onto the verandah at Villa Luna.

"Nobody's going to be arrested," Annabel said with conviction. "We've committed no crime."

"No crime!" Dawn exclaimed, following Annabel into the kitchen. "We've kidnapped a millionaire and threatened to push him out of a plane! We could end up in prison." Grace had lured Hausmann away from his entourage and assorted henchmen, claiming that Cody wanted to talk with him about selling Moon Island. He had gotten quite a shock to find himself face to face with Annabel.

Annabel smiled. "Hausmann is not going to bring charges, trust me."

"Well, why don't you go out there and make sure," Violet said. "I'll brew some tea." She glanced around. "Where do you keep your biscuits, dear?"

Dawn tossed her hands up impatiently. "This is madness. I'm catching the next flight out of here."

"Fine." There was laughter in Annabel's voice. "Are you going straight back to the airstrip or will you join us for tea first?"

Dawn headed for the door. "You've all lost your minds," she declared. "I'm going to see Grace."


GRACE, DON, BEVAN and Cody were gathered in a circle with Robert Hausmann at the center. He looked as pale as he had when he had first spotted Annabel. It would be just their luck if he popped off with a heart attack before they could get him back to Rarotonga, Dawn thought gloomily.

"—so you could view this as an opportunity," Don was saying in a silky voice. "There's enough material in this article to fry your ass permanently. And an attempted murder rap won't do much for your credibility either."

"You can't prove a thing," Hausmann blustered.

"Oh sure," Grace said icily. "You knew Annabel would never sell so you backed right off. Then by some happy coincidence her plane went down. And before she was even reported missing, you had signed a contract with the Japanese to use the island for dumping."

"I can see the front cover of *Time* now," Don said. "'Multinational Mob Tactics. Hausmann Plays Godfather in Pacific Dumping Scandal.' And you had it all worked out at this end, too. A couple of malleable officials are paid to shut up, and the Government has a stake in keeping things quiet. You persuaded them to buy shares at a high. If the deal collapsed, the bottom would fall out of the stock, and the Cooks would be bankrupted."

"I'm sure the Premier will be relieved to know Argus plans to buy back those shares at a premium," Grace added. "I don't know how you're going to explain it to your shareholders, but that's your problem."

"Okay." Hausmann raised a hand. "I'm getting the picture loud and clear. What's your price?" He surveyed them with cynical self-assurance. "Two million and you keep the island. We'll buy some other coconut kingdom. I really don't give a shit."

"Then why not dump in your own back yard for a change, Mr. Hausmann?" Annabel emerged bearing a tray of teacups. Setting them down, she glanced around the small group. "I think that seems reasonable, don't you?"

Hausmann began, "What are you talking about?"

Grace cut him off. "I think she's saying maybe it's time companies like Argus started investing in alternative solutions to waste dumping. Like maybe the people who live here have a few rights, too."

"So tell it to the French and the Japanese. Jesus, it's not my fucking problem. They want a service, we provide it. That's business."

"And murder?" Grace grabbed a handful of his shirt. "Is that business, too? You're in big trouble, Hausmann. And for once you can't buy your way out." With an expression of disgust, she released him and turned to Annabel. "I think we're wasting our time. It's you he nearly killed. What do you want us to do with him? Feed him to the sharks?"

"Tempting," Annabel mused, pouring cups of tea. "But let's not sink to his level. The Dominie was insured, and if it hadn't happened I would never have met Violet. I guess what I really want is some kind of guarantee that Argus will keep out of the Pacific."

"So maybe a public pledge from Argus that it will suspend all toxic dumping activities, a commitment to put a few million into researching alternatives, some significant donations to environmental agencies..." Grace eyeballed Hausmann. "And you buy back that stock from the Cook Islands government. In exchange we'll keep quiet and you'll stay out of prison."

Hausmann was shaking his head. "Impossible. We can't just get out of dumping. The Mexican contracts alone run for another ten years." Don was writing furiously.

"Okay. So you stay out of the Pacific, and you pressure other corporations to do the same," Grace said. "Argus is a major shareholder in a dozen manufacturers that I know are breaching their own countries' environmental protection statutes. I'll be watching for an improvement in their performance."

"You're serious." Hausmann looked incredulous. He shook his head. "Certifiable fucking tree-huggers."

"You finished drafting that agreement?" Grace asked Don.

"I'm not signing anything," Hausmann protested. "Our attorneys..."

"You're screwed, old chap," Bevan said. "Get used to it."

"You're not going to get away with this," Hausmann hissed. "This is not the fucking Magic Kingdom."

"You better hope it is, at 25,000 feet without a parachute," Grace said dryly. "You'll be needing a star to wish upon."

"Milk or lemon?" Annabel asked, handing Dawn a cup of tea as if this was a garden party.

Grace scanned the handwritten document then shoved it in front of Hausmann. "Give the man a pen," she said.

Dawn held her breath. Grace's steely determination brooked no argument. For a long moment Hausmann stared at the agreement in disbelief, then, with a shaking hand, he signed.


"DO YOU THINK we'll get away with it?" Dawn asked that evening on Rarotonga. They had dumped Hausmann beside the Argus jet, waved Violet off on the Silk & Boyd freighter, and were sitting in a conspicuous huddle around a table at the Banana Court.

"We did already." Don fluttered the contract Hausmann signed. "This is witnessed."

Annabel frowned. "We did obtain his signature under duress."

"It was the least he deserved, surely," Grace remarked. "What's a black eye? I wanted to kill the bastard."

Dawn stared at Grace, scandalized at her brazen unconcern. "You'll lose your job," was all she could think to say.

Grace laughed, a low warm sound. "It's a bit late for that, Dawn. I've already resigned."

"You resigned!" Annabel remarked. "I confess I'm touched."

Grace looked wry. "Well, as much as I'd like to take credit where it's not due, the truth is, I was going to quit anyway."

"Tired of environmental sabotage?" Cody's tone fell short of the lightness Dawn guessed she'd attempted.

Grace conceded the point with a slight ironic nod. "I guess deep down even I have a conscience, Cody."

"Well, that calls for a toast," Annabel said and paused a moment while they organized their drinks. "To conscience," she pronounced. "A saving grace in tragically short supply."

As they left the Banana Court, Dawn tugged at Grace's arm.

"Have you really resigned?"

Grace took her hand and kissed the palm. "I guess I forgot to tell you."

Dawn halted in her tracks. "When? When did you decide that?"

Grace's eyes sparkled, her mouth twitched, then she started running.

"Hey! That's not fair!" Dawn hollered after her. "I can't run."

Grace put her hands on her hips and laughed. "So crawl!"

Outraged, Dawn flung her stick aside, negotiated her way through a throng of parked mopeds, and broke into a mutant form of running. "You wait, Grace Ramsay!" she bellowed.

And Grace did.

# Chapter
## Twenty-seven

GRACE RECLINED ON a picnic blanket beneath a group of rustling palms. Late afternoon was her favorite time on Hibiscus Bay. The heat of the day was fading from the grainy white sand, shadows deepened beneath the palm trees, and the sky was bluer than the ocean.

Closing her eyes, she allowed her mind to wander. They were leaving tomorrow; she for the bite of a New York winter, Dawn to Sydney. It would be Mardi Gras time soon. For a moment Grace allowed herself to wallow in envy. Sydney's gay and lesbian community was large and thriving. She remembered her days living there as one endless party, from the Sleaze Ball to the Mardi Gras, the dances, the clubs and bars of Oxford Street. In East Sydney it was easy to forget there was a straight world out there. It was one of the best places in the world to be young, free, and lesbian.

She imagined Dawn finding her feet there, pictured women picking her up, making love with her. She felt sick with jealousy. Grace was all too aware of the contradictory feelings she had for Dawn, feelings she had been trying to sort out ever since the day Annabel disappeared.

It would have been so easy to pick up where she left off. Dawn had a crush on her. Why not enjoy one another for a few months until the sexual tension dissipated? Grace had rejected the idea almost as soon as she contemplated it. She desired Dawn, yet it wasn't just sex she wanted. For a change, a meaningless affair had little appeal. What was the alternative? A white picket fence? *Honey, I'm home...*

With a long sigh, Grace rolled onto her stomach and told herself to get over it. Dawn wasn't her type. She conjured her face, still bearing the last traces of childhood, eyes wide and curious, expression unguarded and at times painfully transparent.

She was far too young, Grace decided, and only just coming

out. It would be a disaster. Dawn would end up hurt, and Grace would end up feeling like a jerk all over again. Grace thought about her warmth and youthful arrogance, the sensitive emotions she disguised with brashness. Dawn had grit, too. The gutsy self-confidence that had made her a champion swimmer had also helped her through her terrible accident. Young she might be, but she had character. Grace liked that. She liked Dawn's honesty, her complete lack of guile.

For a split second Grace indulged herself, recalling Dawn's face suffused with passion, her welcoming mouth. She could almost feel Dawn naked beside her, trembling and responsive. She was Dawn's first lover. It should have been someone else. It should have been a woman who really cared about her. At least Grace could do the decent thing now, by stepping aside so that Dawn was free to find that woman.

Grace jerked abruptly as something cold and wet landed on her back. A sponge. Groping for it, she hurled it at the laughing woman standing over her.

Fending off the soggy missile, Dawn giggled. "I was looking for you." Without further ado, she plunked herself down on the blanket beside Grace and set about removing her clothes.

*God, she was beautiful.* Grace squirmed as her companion prattled on happily about Annabel and Cody, and how crazy she must have been to imagine Annabel would ever cheat. They were so much in love and such a wonderful couple. *So lucky.*

With a pointed look at Grace, Dawn tossed her shirt aside and rubbed sunblock across her naked breasts. There was nothing provocative in her demeanor, yet Grace found herself short of breath. Dawn's clean, sea-washed scent seduced her senses. A thrill of awareness snapped through her.

"My nipples are sore," Dawn complained, examining each of them with dismay. "They must be sunburnt." Carefully she applied lotion to them.

Grace laughed softly. Her own nipples were sore too, but not because of the sun. She was so aroused, her breasts were aching.

"Look," Dawn said, pulling off her shorts and pointing proudly at her more damaged leg. "Muscles."

Grace's gaze slid down the ragged scar, noticing the improved tone and greater fullness. "That's great," she said, clearing her throat. She could hardly take her eyes off Dawn's thighs, the bright triangle of her bikini pants between them.

Dawn was so much less wary of showing her injuries now. Sometimes she seemed completely unconscious of them. She still took painkillers, but less often. Realizing she was staring, Grace looked away.

Dawn seemed to interpret her withdrawal as something more significant. Looking crestfallen, she asked quietly, "Do my legs repel you? Is that why you...we..."

"No. Not at all." Grace ran her fingertips lightly across the scarred flesh. Her hand lingered on Dawn's thigh.

It was not the first time Dawn had alluded to their platonic friendship. During the past few days, she had made a point of seeking Grace out, letting her know in a myriad of ways that she wanted their love-making to resume.

Dawn released a small sound half way between a moan and a sigh and slid down the blanket, closing the gap between them. "Why?" she murmured urgently. "Why don't you want me any more? Please tell me. Was I no good or something?"

"No!" Grace denied emphatically. "You were wonderful." Memories swamped her senses. Dawn hot and wet, clinging to her, crying out in startled ecstasy.

"Then why? Is it because I'm younger?"

"Maybe that's some of it," Grace didn't want to be drawn into this. Noble self-sacrifice had never been her strong suit. She needed to get up right now and walk away from temptation, or her good intentions would pave the proverbial road to hell.

She permitted her arm to drift around Dawn's waist, planning to tell her as gently as she could that she would be better off finding someone closer in age, someone who would love her the way she deserved to be loved. "Dawn, I still desire you," she said. "I never stopped. But—"

"No buts." Dawn removed her sunglasses and stretched a hand to Grace's face, sliding her fingers into her hair. She brushed Grace's mouth with her own, whispering, "I've missed you so much. Please make love to me."

Their kisses deepened. Unfastening Grace's shirt, Dawn slipped her hands beneath the soft cotton, drawing Grace closer until their bodies were perfectly aligned. Her hands felt tentative against Grace's back, delicately caressing her prickling flesh. They stared at one another, breathing hard.

Grace's heartbeat gathered speed. "I've missed you, too," she said, knowing this was her last chance. If she didn't walk away now, she was going to take Dawn Beaumont to bed and to hell with the consequences.

"Your place or mine?" Dawn asked, as if Grace's compliance was a foregone conclusion.

And she was right. Grace hesitated for less than a second, and said. "You choose, baby."

Without another word they got up and walked hand-in-hand

into the jungle, leaving their blanket and clothing languishing beneath the tropical sun.


DAWN LOOKED NERVOUS as they entered her bedroom, but she turned to Grace and moved into her waiting arms. Grace kissed her slowly, and they all but collapsed onto the bed. For a long time they lay still, locked in an embrace that was replete with emotion—relief, passion, tenderness, anticipation. The heat of their bodies soon transformed to moisture, and they slithered against one another, thighs intertwined, hands caressing, mouths tasting.

Grace felt wild laughter rise inside her at the sheer delight of Dawn's touch. Nerves dancing beneath her skin, she kissed and licked her way past the full damp breasts she had missed so much, over Dawn's rounded belly, down to the fine blonde hair that divided her thighs. Dawn gasped with delight as Grace slid an arm beneath her, lifting her slightly and capturing her clit delicately between her teeth. Exerting the very slightest pressure, she teased the tiny bud into swollen awareness, ceasing only when she could feel Dawn's arousal climbing steeply.

Grazing her tongue over skin as smooth as watered silk, she traced a sensuous path down to the salty, yielding opening, the secret passage they had shared with such intensity. As Grace buried her tongue there, Dawn's legs closed around her head, imprisoning her. For a long while, Grace was content to respond to the demands of Dawn's body, giving what she had withheld, building a bridge of sensation she could cross at will. Soon she would take Dawn home, right over the edge. But not yet.

She wanted to linger, to cherish every inch of this woman, to savor every moment of their lovemaking as if it might be the last. Yet at the same time, she wanted to lose herself mindlessly in the honeyed trap of passion.

Grace turned her face to the pliant flesh of Dawn's inner thighs, licking and biting softly. She found the knit of scar tissue, puckering the polished satin of Dawn's skin, and followed it tenderly along her leg. The younger woman stiffened at first, then relaxed as Grace claimed ownership of her most sensitive self.

"Please," she whispered, quivering and hot. "Now. Please Grace."

Grace drew back, drinking in the sight of Dawn's flushed cheeks, her eyes damp and dark with arousal. "You're beautiful."

Taking Dawn in her arms, Grace lifted her to a kneeling

position, and, facing one another, they moved as if joined, bodies and mouths aligned. Grace paused in her caresses, gasping when Dawn's teeth sank into her shoulder. Fiercely, she twisted her fingers into Dawn's hair, pulling her head back to expose her throat. Controlling an urge to devour the sweet hollow at its base, she gently kissed her way around the column of her neck, finding the hot, wild pulse beating as crazily as her own.

Dawn's breathing came in short harsh bursts, and her skin glowed pinkly. She murmured hoarse little pleas as Grace covered her shoulders in soft bites and licked the film of moisture collecting between her breasts.

Seizing Grace's hand, Dawn guided it determinedly between her thighs, where her soft pale hair was matted with her juices. "Please." She gripped Grace's shoulders for balance. "I can't bear it."

With a sense of awe, Grace drove her fingers inside Dawn, and the rhythm of their lovemaking altered sharply. From somewhere deep in Dawn's throat a low sound emerged. Wracked by a series of deep shudders, Dawn sagged against Grace, and they both collapsed onto the sheets, laughing between wild kisses.

Limp and panting, they floated in the liquid aftermath of pleasure. Grace could not remember how she ended up on her back, but suddenly Dawn was kneeling over her, gripping her shoulders. "I love you," she said, running her hands across Grace's breasts. "Tell me what you want."

Grace took Dawn's hands, drew them to her mouth and kissed the fingers with sensual deliberation. There was a time when she could have answered that question in precise technical detail, but it felt like a thousand years ago now. For a split second she felt fearful, reluctant to expose herself. Then she smiled and said, "It's you I want, Dawn. Today. Tomorrow. Always."

# Epilogue

THREE MONTHS LATER on Passion Bay, Cody announced, "It's a letter from Dawn. Want me to read out the best bits?"

Annabel peered out from beneath the brim of her hat. "It's not another description of some DJ at that club is it? I think I'm getting old."

"No, they're in Sydney now. Grace got a job with Greenpeace. Who would have thought?" Cody scanned the letter. "Dawn came out to her folks. She says they're still praying."

"That's nice, dear."

"The cops in New York have a suspect and the DNA matches. Grace described the other men to the sketch artist, too." Cody read on. "She's seeing a therapist."

"All good news."

"Dawn wants to borrow the B-17."

Annabel raised her eyebrows. "Excuse me?"

"She's been taking flying lessons."

"God help us."

"She wants to know how easy it is to skywrite."

"Dare I ask why?"

"For the Mardi Gras next year," Cody enthused. "She wants to paint a rainbow flag over Sydney."

Also available from
*Yellow Rose Books*

# Passion Bay

*Book I in the Moon Island Series*
(2nd edition)

Two women from different ends of the earth meet in paradise. Mourning the death of her favorite Aunt, Annabel Worth is stunned to find she has inherited two things—an island in the South Pacific and a mystery that can only be solved by traveling there. Disillusioned with life as a securities trader in Boston, she rashly decides to exchange one world for another. New Zealander Cody Stanton has made the same choice. Dumped by her lover, laid off from her job, she rents a beach villa on remote Moon Island, expecting to take comfort in sea, solitude and simplicity. Then she meets Annabel.

Haunted by a secret that threatens to derail her relationship with her mother, Annabel resists their powerful attraction. Cody, too, is burdened with a secret that could destroy the passion growing between them. When Hurricane Mary strikes the island, each woman must make a choice that will change her life forever.

A runaway bestseller with seven reprints in its first edition, *Passion Bay* has been re-released in a second 'author's cut' edition, extensively revised, updated and expanded.

**Here's what the critics say:** "Send your customers looking for the perfect beach book to *Passion Bay*...this novel absolutely has it all." ~ Feminist Bookstore News

ISBN 1-932300-25-2

Other Jennifer Fulton books to look for in the coming
months from
*Yellow Rose Books*

# *The Sacred Shore*

## *Book III in the Moon Island Series*

A page-turning journey packed with romance, adventure,
humor, spirituality and steamy eroticism. Third in this unfor-
gettable series, *The Sacred Shore* brings together a group of
women at crossroads in their lives. Successful tech industry
survivor, Merris Randall does not believe in love at first sight
until she meets Olivia Pearce. But Olivia is deeply scarred
from a damaging relationship, and has no plans to love again.
Thrown together in a sensuous paradise thousands of miles
from home, each comes face to face with her destiny. Anthro-
pologist Dr. Glenn Howick is also on Moon Island, but
romance is not on her agenda. Chasing the career-making discovery of a lifetime, Glenn must decide whether she can
exploit the spirituality of another culture for her own ends.
Another moral dilemma looms in the form of her research
assistant Riley Mason, a post-grad student whose love for
Glenn threatens both her reputation and her most secret self.

After five years of bliss, life seems complete for the
island's owners, Cody and Annabel. At least Cody thinks so.
But Annabel has recently woken up to the sound of her biolog-
ical clock ticking. With preparations underway for the secret
rituals local women perform to celebrate the goddess of the
island, the topic is consigned to the back burner. Then Annabel's cousin Melanie shows up with a young baby and a desperate problem.

# A Guarded Heart

## Book IV in the Moon Island Series

In her life Lauren Douglas never imagined she would wake up one day and find herself the star of the hottest soap on daytime television. But as wholesome, smart and lovely Dr. Kate, she is plastered over the media as a role model and inspiration for young women. As she is about to sign a bloated new contract, Lauren is publicly outed. Scrambling for damage control, her father, a Congressman, wants her banished abroad and her network writes her temporarily out of the show in a plane crash, while they consider her future. As if the slavering press doesn't have enough to report, a creepy fan enraged by the revelation, shoots her. All of which means zip to FBI Special Agent Pat Roussel whose hunt for the Kiddy Pageant Killer has consumed every waking moment for three years. Suffering from burnout, and hoping fresh new eyes might come up with a break in the case, Pat reluctantly elects to take a few months leave without pay. The last thing she expects to find herself doing in her time off is an illicit private security gig babysitting a celebrity. But she owes a friend a big favor. Her first assignment sounds like hell-a month on a tropical island as bodyguard for a TV star with a bullet wound. Only Lauren is not the spoiled narcissist Pat is expecting.

Jennifer Fulton lives in the shadow of the Rocky Mountains with her partner and animal companions. Her vice of choice is writing, however she is also devoted to her wonderful daughter and her hobbies: fly fishing, film, and fine cooking. Jennifer started writing stories almost as soon as she could read them, and never stopped. Under pen names Jennifer Fulton and Rose Beecham, she has published seven lesbian novels and a handful of short stories.

Printed in the United States
45486LVS00005B/122